Pursuing

Justice

A JOURNEY OF INTEGRITY, LOVE AND LAW

JOHN RUSSELL

HOJOPRESS PUBLISHING

ISBN: 979-8-9923636-0-9 (paperback)

Book design by : Angle Moni

www.hojopresspublishing.com

For my wife Holli,

Your integrity and unwavering authenticity light my way every day. You inspire me not only through the strength of your character but with your fierce dedication to being true to yourself, no matter what the world expects. Thank you for being my constant source of courage and for showing me, through all things, the beauty of a life lived with purpose and heart.

Prologue

I n pursuing our dreams, we often find ourselves at the crossroads
of ambition and purpose, wrestling with the delicate balance
between achieving success and remaining true to our values. This
journey is not merely a personal struggle; it is a shared experience
that unites us in our quest for justice and integrity in a world that
sometimes seems indifferent to our ideals.

We often face challenges that test our resilience and perseverance.
The weight of expectations—both external and internal—can be
overwhelming. In our ambition to excel, we may question whether we
are sacrificing too much of who we are for success. This conflict can
be particularly pronounced for those who frequently navigate societal
pressures to prove themselves in their careers while also maintaining
personal integrity.

This book tells the story of Holli Bauchman, a woman whose
journey reflects the complexities many of us face. Her fight for justice
highlights the importance of standing firm in our principles, even
when the stakes are high. Her experiences show us how perseverance

and resilience can lead us through dark moments and inspire us to rise above adversity.

But more than an entertaining story, it reminds us that we are not alone in our struggles. It resonates with anyone who has grappled with the question of what it means to pursue ambition without losing sight of our purpose. It invites readers to reflect on their lives, encouraging them to embrace their journeys and find strength in their convictions.

We are reminded that true fulfillment lies not in what we achieve but in how we navigate our paths with integrity and purpose. This is a story for anyone who has ever stood at the intersection of ambition and values, urging us to honor our aspirations while remaining true to ourselves.

Contents

1. Chapter 1   1

2. Chapter 2   11

3. Chapter 3   17

4. Chapter 4   27

5. Chapter 5   35

6. Chapter 6   49

7. Chapter 7   59

8. Chapter 8   69

9. Chapter 9   79

10. Chapter 10   91

11. Chapter 11   105

12. Chapter 12   121

Acknowledgements   129

About the author   131

Chapter 1

I adjusted my rearview mirror with a practiced flick of my wrist. My reflection was a testament to years of tireless dedication etched in the lines of my face. The dark circles under my eyes spoke of countless late nights deciphering contracts, each a new challenge to unravel. I had just lost a case—a lawsuit I was sure would go my way. Tears started to fall on my face. I took my hand and wiped them away.

I began to drive. I was going from my office at Winston and Associates, and the drive was familiar. I began to look around Sunnyville's beautiful ocean views.

Nestled within the cradle of rolling hills, Sunnyville sprawled beneath a canopy of verdant slopes. The wind whispered through the leaves, harmonizing with the gentle murmur of a nearby stream, creating a tranquil backdrop for the town's idyllic setting. Along the quaint street, life pulsed with vibrant energy. Locals bustled about, laughter mingling with footsteps on cobblestone pathways, a joyous symphony that resonated through the air.

I drove with the convertible top down, my long black hair flowing in the breeze. I was still wearing the same clothes from court, the heels giving me a bit of extra height over my usual 5'4" frame.

In Sunnyville, community was not a concept, but an ingrained way of life. Bonds between residents ran deep, forged through shared experiences and unwavering support. The people stood together with loyalty and love, celebrating life's joys or weathering storms.

A memory from high school surfaced in my mind. The journey toward a law career began with a poignant incident involving a friend. Despite her innocence, she faced unjust punishment from the administration. The administrators' negligence resulted in severe consequences for her. Witnessing it sparked a profound sense of unfairness within me and ignited a strong desire to combat biased treatment. This early experience became a pivotal moment, shaping my understanding of the critical importance of fairness and impartiality.

In college, I volunteered at a local clinic that served marginalized communities struggling with predatory lending practices perpetuated by unregulated financial institutions. Each day, I picked up sad stories of individuals trapped in the relentless cycles of debt and exploitation.

One of the cases that left a lasting impression was that of Mr. Nguyen. He was an elderly man who signed a subprime mortgage with hidden fees and adjustable rates beyond his fixed income. What started as a dream of homeownership turned into a nightmare of impending foreclosure. It threatened to strip away the stability he worked so hard to achieve in his later years.

A few years ago, I took a pro bono job representing a group of immigrant workers—victims of wage theft by a construction company. Through diligent work and steadfast advocacy, I worked through complex labor laws and secured clients compensation. Seeing the positivity that justice brought to their lives, helped me see why I wanted to pursue a career in law.

I had some extra time, so I stopped to collect my thoughts. My footsteps echoed on the cobblestones as I strolled through the park. The sky was painted in hues of amber and crimson across the grassy expanse. A bench beneath a towering oak tree drew me in, branches reaching upward like ancient sentinels.

Seating myself, I sighed, recalling a conversation with my mentor, Denise Jackson, years ago. We sat right here, discussing the law's intricacies. Wise with weathered hands, she spoke about her experiences.

"The path to partnership is fraught with challenges, Holli," she said, pride and caution in her voice. "You must be prepared to make sacrifices—time, personal life, sometimes even your principles."

This promotion was nothing but a distant mirage for me – one that promised success and validation for my career.

Laughter.

Children laughing, nearby.

It pulled me from my thoughts...Children chasing one another, oblivious to adult complexities—career choices, trade-offs, and responsibilities.

Closing my eyes, I pondered my journey—fighting cases, winning victories, and enduring losses. Each step brought me closer to this moment when the path ahead was clear, yet uncertain.

Opening my eyes, I glanced at the oak tree, its roots buried deep. The oak tree is a symbol of resilience. Could I find that rootedness in my job amidst tumultuous battles and personal aspirations?

The sun dipped below the horizon, casting long shadows, I made a silent vow; I'll pursue the law with unwavering determination, without losing myself. Partnership in the firm may be a goal, but not at the expense of my values and the deeper.

Twilight turned to night, and I was in my car, heading to dinner. The recent case lingered in my mind. A family faced homelessness, and despite my meticulous efforts, I couldn't overcome the hurdles in time to prevent their eviction. Their despair was evident, their future uncertain—a stark reminder of the real-life consequences of outcomes.

The impact of losing extends beyond the courtroom. It weighed on my conscience, questioning if I could have done more. Suppose I could have explored more angles. It fueled a sense of frustration and determination to learn from setbacks, innovate, and find new approaches to address the issues in a broken system.

I experienced the gravity of this loss. It's more than just the case, it's about the lives affected by it. Families struggling to maintain their homes and individuals standing up for justice rely on me.

Having partners witness my performance in court adds to the pressure. They recognized how I presented and delivered my closing arguments to the jury, which was pivotal since my specialty is contracts.

The thought that my aspirations to partner in this prestigious law firm might not materialize weighed on me, plunging me into a profound state of reflection.

Every victory I've achieved, kept me going. From helping wrongfully convicted defendants to supporting employees facing workplace discrimination, I've seen the impact of courage and resilience firsthand.

While systemic inequality is still a challenge, every case I worked on helped me understand its purpose—to restore the dignity of the wronged and hold offenders accountable. It helped me build trust in the system's power to bring positive change."

The radio played, and the music lifted my spirits. I had always loved to sing. My idea of the perfect night out was to go to a karaoke bar and sing the night away. Smooth jazz flowed from my favorite station. I recognized the song and began singing along, trying to shake off the funk from losing. I needed to be in a good mood tonight; I was heading to the beach.

I was on my way to meet my boyfriend, John Knox. He and I met during an independent investigation my friends and I worked on. He is a detective at the Sunnyville Police Department, and we require his expertise. I guess he was smitten because he asked me out not long after. Our relationship started strong. We grew close, almost inseparable, in those early days. His work always intrigued me, and he was curious about the aspects of our cases. We had a great connection.

He was a stern man, but his love was always clear. I remember the day he told me why he chose law enforcement. We sat in his study, the low hum of the ceiling fan barely cutting through the thick summer heat. His face was calm, though his eyes carried something heavy.

"Why'd you do it?" I asked, leaning forward in my chair. "Why'd you become a cop?"

He sat still momentarily, staring past me like people do when reaching for a memory. "I was about ten," he started, voice low. "There was a man who broke into our house."

I blinked, caught off guard. He had never mentioned this before.

"It was just me and my mom that night," he continued, his fingers tapping lightly on the armrest. "We lived in a rough neighborhood. She worked late, and I was alone most of the time. One night, someone kicked in the front door." He paused, his jaw tightening.

"What happened?" I asked, feeling the tension in the room shift.

"I hid," he said, his voice steady but distant. "Behind the couch. I could hear him going through our things, smashing plates and drawers being yanked out. Mom came home while he was still there. He grabbed her before she could even scream."

His fists clenched on his lap. I could picture the scene as he described it: his small frame trembling, curled up behind the couch, heart racing.

"I thought... I thought he was going to kill her." His breath hitched slightly, but he kept his gaze steady on the floor. "But then, the cops showed up. A neighbor or someone passerby must've called them. They busted in, guns drawn, and I saw the officer pull that man off my mom. He saved her life. That day, I decided I'd do the same for someone else's family."

I didn't know what to say. His story explained everything—the long hours, the nights he came home quiet, staring at the walls.

"Years later," he continued, "when I got my badge, I told myself I'd always be that officer. The one who shows up in time."

I nodded—the silence between us felt thick, like neither wanted to disturb it. Then, he shifted in his seat, breaking the moment.

"Which brings me to the mission," he said, clearing his throat. "Have you ever heard about the Belridge standoff?"

I shook my head. He leaned back, eyes narrowing slightly as he recounted the story.

"Three men held up in a warehouse," he said. "Armed. Hostages. We had no intel on their plan, only that they were willing to kill if provoked. SWAT was called, but the clock was ticking. They had a little girl in there—maybe eight or nine. It reminded me of that night when I was ten. All I could think about was getting her out alive."

I listened, breath held, as he described the chaos. Officers positioned around the building, trying to negotiate and keep things from spiraling. The tension in the air was palpable, the kind that makes every second feel like an hour.

"SWAT couldn't wait anymore," he continued. "We got the signal to move in. My heart was pounding like it hadn't since the academy. I kicked down that door... and there she was. In the middle of it all. Terrified, clutching a doll like it was the only thing keeping her grounded."

He swallowed hard, and I saw it in his eyes. He was back there, in that room, seeing the little girl. "I grabbed her, got her out, and before I knew it, we had the gunmen down."

I sat there, feeling the weight of his story settle between us. He ran his hand through his hair, exhaling slowly like the memory had released something he'd kept locked away for a while.

"That's why I do this job," he said, glancing at me. "It's not about the badge or authority. It's about showing up when nobody else can."

I felt relieved by his dedication to helping others in difficult situations. "Thank you for what you do," I said, reaching across the table to squeeze his hand.

I parked my car at the beautiful restaurant overlooking the water. My personal life began weighing on my mind. Through the window, I spotted John. The vibrant energy of our shared dreams and aspirations gave way to a sad stillness. Each moment was tinged with the bittersweet sting of missed opportunities.

I stepped out of the vehicle, the evening breeze carrying the salty scent of the ocean, a stark contrast to the turmoil in my heart. He was seated at a corner table, staring at the waves.

I strolled towards the table. He offered a small, tentative smile, and pulled out my chair. "Hi, Holli."

I sat down. "Thanks for meeting me here."

He nodded, sitting back down. "Of course. How have you been?"

I sighed, folding my hands. "It's been. I lost today."

His brow furrowed with concern. "I'm sorry. You always give it your all—more than most. Don't forget that."

I managed to smile. "Thank you, that means a lot. But, I could handle it. I wish things were different, you know? Like, less chaotic. More... us.

He replied, "I miss it too...miss us. Do you think we've drifted apart? What transpired between us?" He leaned forward, his gaze intense, and continues, "Do you think we can fix this?"

"I don't know." I looked down at my feet, not wanting to look him in the eye.

"Why not?" He shifted in his seat, frustration creeping into his tone. "Why can't we just try?"

"It's not that simple," I replied, a lump forming in my throat. "We're not the same people we were."

"Are you saying it's over?" His voice hardened, the edge of disbelief sharpening his features.

"I'm not saying that. But things have changed. I have changed." My hands clenched in my lap.

My phone buzzed on the table. It was a text from my colleague updating me on a new development. I read the message, realizing that a crucial piece of evidence had been overlooked.

He gazed at my eyes. "Is everything alright?" he asked, his voice tinged with concern.

I shook my head. "No, it's not. We missed something important. It could have changed the outcome."

John's brow furrowed. "I'm sorry, Holli. You can't blame yourself for what goes wrong."

"It's not just that. It's everything. The pressure, the expectations, the constant perception of failing."

The silence was oppressive, and understanding began to bridge the gap between us. The waves outside crashed against the shore, a soothing backdrop to our tense moment.

Navigating this fractured relationship is a delicate balancing act. I wondered if our bond was strong enough to endure or would be swept away by diverging paths.

Chapter 2

I awoke with lingering emotions from Friday's case and my evening with John. Sunday morning, I followed my usual routine. I poured myself a cup of coffee and stepped onto the back porch. The salty scent of the ocean greeted me. Seagulls cried overhead and the distant sound of waves crashing provided a soothing backdrop.

I savored my morning and took in the view. My phone buzzed on the table. I hesitated, reluctant to disrupt the peaceful moment. I answered the call, and to my surprise, it was my brother, Steve. I finished my sip of java.

I smiled. "Hey."

"How's it going?" he said. I could tell, by the tone of his voice, he was excited

I took another drink of my brew. "It's well. I am just enjoying myself on the patio. What's up with you?".

"We're moving to Sunnyville!" he said.

"My town?" I sat up in my chair. "That's amazing! When is this happening?"

"In a couple of months. Tiffany got a job offer, and we thought it was a good opportunity for the family."

"That's fantastic. How about the kids?"

"They're thrilled. They're already planning all the places they want to explore."

I got up from the spot on my porch, and went inside and settled on the sofa in my living room. "Sunnyville's got so much to see...Have you found a place to live yet?

"No, but we've been looking at a few neighborhoods. We need one with exceptional schools and a strong sense of community," his voice tinged with enthusiasm.

"That sounds like a smart strategy," I imagined them settling into their home with Steve building a swing set. "How's Tiffany about the move?"

"She's thrilled. She's already started planning and researching all Sunnyville offers."

I took a sip of coffee. "I'm so happy for you. It's going to be such an adventure. How soon?"

"We're aiming for early fall. It gives us time to sort everything out and settle in before the school year starts."

"I can't wait to come visit your house!"

"You're welcome anytime," he said.

"I'm close by if you need anything."

"Thanks, Holli."

I sat up in the chair. "Of course. I'm here for you always. Sunnyville is lucky to have the whole family coming their way."

"I'm glad we caught up like this. It's been too long," he said, his voice hinting nostalgia.

"Me too." I was thankful for the uplifting conversation.

We ended the call, and I smiled. Having him nearby was the best news in ages. Being an aunt to his children meant the world to me. It also gave me an opportunity to bond with Tiffany. The idea of gaining a relationship with my sister-in-law was appealing.

Finishing my coffee, and I pondered what to wear for church. I chose an outfit, I hopped into the shower and got ready while the Lord's miracles unfolded. Brighter days were on the horizon, and I saw His guiding hand in every detail of my day.

Sunday, though, I dedicated the afternoon to assisting Justin Ford—a local hero, receiver for the Emerald City Thunderhawks, and my friend since we met at a charity event. With his charity, the Youth Sports and Education Alliance, a football stadium for our high school was built.

It was his proudest achievement. His dedication was evident, and the team's record improved from 3-6 to 6-3, missing the state playoffs. He attended all the games, delivering a motivational speech in the locker room before the first game. His words worked wonders, propelling the Sunnyville Spartans to a 24-13 victory.

I approached him. His face lit up with a grin. "I'm glad you are here," he said, extending a hand in greeting. "Your help means a lot to us."

I shook his hand, matching his enthusiasm. "Of course. This field is amazing. You've made a difference here."

He nodded, his eyes reflecting pride. "Thanks. It's been a labor of love, seeing how it's brought the community together."

"The team's performance has been incredible. That first game was proof of your leadership."

He chuckled. "They're a talented bunch. We're hoping to build on this success next season."

Giving him a quick smile, I said, "I have no doubt. How can I help today?"

Justin outlined a few tasks for the volunteers, emphasizing teamwork and efficiency. The conversation flowed as we worked, blending updates on the field's maintenance with memories of our community's support.

We stood there in the fading light, he glanced at me, taking a deep breath. "You know, I wasn't sure how today would go," he admitted, his voice a bit softer now that the busyness of the day was behind us. "But seeing how everything came together... it feels good. Better than I expected."

I smiled, sensing the mixture of relief and pride in his tone. "I get that. Sometimes these things start off feeling like chaos, but once everyone finds their rhythm, it just... works. And seeing the impact—well, that's what makes it all worth it."

He looked out toward the emptying stadium, the seats now scattered with just a few lingering shadows. "It's more than just the event, though," he continued, his gaze thoughtful. "It's about showing up, you know? People giving their time, coming together. It's something special."

"Yeah. It's easy to forget how much even small efforts can matter. But days like today? They remind you of it all."

He chuckled softly, his expression lightening. "Exactly. I kept thinking, 'What if no one shows up? What if this doesn't make a difference?' But I look around now, and it's clear—it did."

I gave him a reassuring smile. "You've got nothing to worry about there. The turnout was great...and the energy? That was because of you. People feel that, and they respond to it." I glanced at him. "You and Brittany should swing by for a BBQ at my place sometime soon,"

"You bet I will," He smiled.

"Introducing you two was a good choice. I'm glad you hit it off."

"Goodbye." He waved.

I returned to my car and drove towards home. Pulling into the driveway, I felt a sense of relief. Today, I had a reprieve from Friday's stress. Once inside, I poured a glass of wine and settled in for a quiet evening.

Chapter 3

S tepping into the hallway to my office, the morning air felt heavy.
Framed accolades and certificates lining the walls, reflecting in
the polished floors, marked the firm's legacy. Muted conversation and
ringing phones created a steady rhythm of urgency and order in the
space.

Amanda stood by my door, holding a cup of coffee. Her poised
expression hinted at something beyond the usual morning routine.
"Good morning, Holli." She smiled, her energy unshaken by the early
hour.

"Morning." I reached for the coffee, nodding my thanks.

She motioned toward my desk. "Markson files are ready. Mr.
Reynolds will be here at ten for the new contract terms."

"Great," I said, settling into my chair. Amanda's efficiency was the
engine that kept everything moving.

Her expression shifted, more serious now. She glanced toward the
hallway and leaned in. "Davis wants you in his office. It's about the
football stadium."

I raised an eyebrow. "The stadium?"

"There are rumors about Titan Construction. Environmental violations. Something about the water."

A sharp jolt of unease passed through me. "The stadium? Water contamination? That could ruin Justin's charity."

"It's urgent," she said, her voice low.

I stood, smoothing my jacket. "Let's go."

The walk to Davis's office was brisk, the weight of the rumors pressing on me. The idea of water contamination at a community cornerstone—and the impact on Justin's work—made my chest tighten.

Amanda knocked, and Davis's deep voice called us in.

"Morning, ladies," he said, gesturing toward the chairs across from his desk.

Amanda and I sat. The room smelled of coffee and leather. Davis leaned back, hands clasped, his brow furrowed.

"I got a call last night from Titan Construction." He slid a thick folder across the desk. "The city has sued for environmental concerns—contaminated water at the stadium. Titan blames TerraGuard Technologies, their subcontractor, for environmental compliance. Billings & Boyer represents them."

I opened the folder, flipping through inspection reports and compliance summaries. My fingers brushed the edges of highlighted lines, inconsistencies leaping from the pages.

"What's the plan for the Youth Sports and Education Alliance?" My voice was steady, but the words carried weight. "They rely on that stadium. This could devastate their funding and reputation."

"We focus on Titan," Davis said, his tone sharp. "They're our client. Handle this quickly. Your expertise in contracts and compliance makes you the best for this. It's straightforward—negotiate, settle, and keep it out of court."

Amanda glanced at me, her eyes catching the shift in my posture. My jaw tightened, but I nodded.

"Straightforward," I repeated, closing the folder. "I'll get started."

The air outside Davis's office felt lighter, though my mind raced.

"Pull everything we have on Titan," I said, quickening my pace toward my office. "I need to know what we're walking into. Compliance records, contracts, and anything that ties them to TerraGuard. If Titan is at fault, we'll see it."

Amanda didn't hesitate. "On it."

Hours passed in a blur of papers and screens. Amanda returned, her arms full of documents. She set them on the desk, her usual calm edged with urgency.

"These are the initial reports," she said, smoothing the top sheet. "Skipped inspections, material substitutions, missed audits. TerraGuard cut corners."

I scanned the pages, my eyes narrowing at the flagged sections. "Looks like TerraGuard went cheap on materials. These test results..." I held up a page. "Water quality violations. Non-compliance with waste protocols. It's all here."

I reached for the contract between Titan and TerraGuard. The black-and-white language offered little room for interpretation. "This clause—environmental protections. And here, waste management protocols." I tapped the page. "TerraGuard didn't adhere to either."

Amanda pulled out a highlighter, marking sections as we cross-referenced the reports with the contract. The evidence stacked higher with each passing hour.

"This provision alone is enough for breach," I said, setting the pen down. "If they overlooked this much on paper, imagine what we'll find on-site."

Amanda straightened, determination in her posture. "We'll know for sure tomorrow."

Justin's charity, the community, and Titan's reputation—they all hung in the balance. Whatever we uncovered next could change everything.

The sun beat down on the sprawling grounds as Amanda and I arrived for our inspection. Despite its impressive facade, the knowledge of potential environmental risks loomed over us.

"It's hard to believe this place may have hidden problems." Amanda's voice was concerned as we passed through the bustling entry gates.

I scanned the surroundings. "It can be deceiving. Let's start by checking the drainage systems and areas where runoff might occur."

We began near the stadium's periphery, where rainwater and channels were crucial areas of concern. We couldn't find any signs of contamination— no discoloration in basins, suspicious odors, or sparse vegetation.

Amanda pointed to the section where water from the parking lot entered a stream. "This area is vulnerable."

I jotted down notes for further investigation. "Let's collect specimens from here and a few other strategic points. We need a clearer picture of what's happening beneath the surface."

Workers continued their tasks as we moved deeper into the grounds, oblivious to our scrutiny. Remaining discreet while gathering evidence was essential to avoid causing undue alarm among staff and visitors.

By mid-day, we had collected water samples from designated locations. Each sample would undergo rigorous testing to determine the presence and levels of contaminants—critical data that would inform our next steps.

A familiar voice called out behind us as Amanda and I wrapped up our inspection near the stadium's west wing. "Holli! What brings you both out here today?"

Justin's trademark grin lit up his face despite the seriousness of our current investigation.

I smiled at him. "Good, you are here." My mind raced over how to broach the sensitive topic of water contamination.

Amanda stepped forward, her professional demeanor unwavering. "We're conducting a routine assessment of environmental conditions around here."

Justin's expression turned. "I received a call from my attorneys today. I had to come down here and see for myself if there is any evidence of potential issues."

I hesitated for a moment, choosing my words. "Concerns have been raised, but we're investigating to ensure Titian followed the highest standards."

He understood the gravity of the situation. "The charity relies on this stadium. If there's anything I can do to help..."

"Your perspective would be invaluable," Amanda said, her gaze steady. "You know how this impacts the community. Any information you provide or share might assist us in our assessment."

Justin's eyes brightened. "I understand. Well, I haven't seen changes in the water quality. I appreciate all you're doing. Don't hesitate to ask if you need anything else from me or the charity."

I looked at him. "Thank you. We'll keep you updated on our progress."

He walked away and Amanda glanced at me. I was grateful for Justin's support and insight. "Let's make sure we include him in our communication moving forward. I don't want to mess up our relationship."

We drove back to Winston and Associates to review the day's findings. The samples would need to be analyzed. Our initial observations pointed to potential issues with runoff management and the stadium's impact on local water quality.

Amanda was thumbing a pencil on my desk.

"The completed construction complicates things," I said, reviewing the photos of drainage areas on my computer screen. "We must strategize to address this without disrupting stadium operations."

Amanda drew closer. "Perhaps we should consider partnering with engineers to conduct a comprehensive assessment? They may help us develop a plan that minimizes disruption while ensuring the safety of the surrounding environment."

I recognized the need for expert input to navigate the complexities of mitigating impacts post-construction. "Let's reach out to a few firms.

On my drive home, John's silence weighed on me. The case was crucial for my career. We had made strides, and were confident we could build a solid defense for Titian Construction. I had the just received notice that TerraGuard filed a defemination suit against Titan and Bill McAllister. It hung over me like a storm cloud. I knew that if I did a timely and complete job, I would be up for a partnership which made the stakes high. Reputations and livelihoods made the stakes higher. I had to remind myself to breathe, to take it one issue at a time. Any misstep could unravel everything, so I couldn't afford to get overwhelmed. Focus, I told myself. Just handle what's in front of you.

I stood by the bay window of my home. The city lights twinkling below. My phone buzzed on the coffee table; it was John. I hesitated before answering, my heart was heavy.

Attempting to keep my voice steady, I spoke first. "Hey."

"Hi," he responded.

I let out a slow breath, hoping to ease the tension. "So... how was your day?"

"Pretty packed," he said, his tone a bit stiff. Then, after a pause, "We need to talk."

A knot tightened in my stomach. "Okay," I replied, bracing myself.

He exhaled. "It feels like we're... out of sync these days."

I nodded, keeping my voice as steady as I could. "Yeah. I've felt that, too."

He leaned forward, the frustration still there but a little softened. "It's like every time we try to talk, it somehow spirals into... this."

I managed a small smile. "An argument?"

A short laugh escaped him despite himself. "Exactly. It's like we're not even speaking the same language."

Sadness surged in my thoughts. "I thought we were building something, but we're growing separately."

"You don't understand it from my side," John said. "I desire someone who's there, who gets me."

I bit my upper lip. "I love you, but How do we make this better? Like it was."

Silence hung heavily between us before he finally spoke again.

"I love you too," he said. "We need time apart."

Teardrops welled up in my eyes, but I blinked them back. "I'm sorry," I said. "I truly am."

He paused for a moment. "I'm sorry, too, for everything."

Unable to hold them back any longer, tears rolled down my cheeks, "I will miss you."

"I will miss you too."

We said our goodbyes, a strange mix of sorrow and relief was in the air. Letting go was painful, but acknowledging the truth also gave us a sense of freedom. We both needed to move forward.

I stood by the window, feeling the weight of our conversation. The city lights below blurred into a haze and my thoughts swirled with sadness.

I replayed our words in my mind, each a sharp reminder of how far we had wandered from each other. The room became emptier now, the silence punctuated only by the occasional passing car outside. I wanted to reach out to him again, to close the space that had widened between us. I realized deep down that some distances were beyond my control.

With a heavy sigh, I turned away from the window and wandered around my house. Every corner held memories of us—laughter shared over dinner, quiet moments of comfort on the couch, and late-night conversations that once warmed me.

The ache in my heart remained. I needed to speak with someone. I got my phone and called my good friend Samantha.

After the first ring, she picked up. "Hi Holli."

"Hey." A familiar voice comforted me. "How have you been?"

"Oh, busy as ever," she said. "I am exhausted but hanging in there. What about you? How's everything going?"

I felt my shoulders tense. "It's been a rollercoaster, to be honest. I have a case progressing that needs my full attention, but things are finished for John and me."

Samantha's tone softened. "I'm sorry about that."

I sat back on the sofa. "We had a conversation earlier, it didn't go well and we called it quits."

There was a pause on the other end of the line, filled with unspoken concern. "I'm here for you, Holli. Do you want to talk about it?"

I hesitated. "I don't know where to start. We're on different pages and I don't understand how to bridge the gap."

"I'm sure it's difficult," Samantha empathized. "Perhaps talking it out will help. Sometimes saying things aloud can bring clarity."

"Yeah, you're right. Thanks. I needed that." I adjusted the phone against my ear.

"Anytime, one step at a time."

"Thanks," I said. "I appreciate you listening."

"Of course. That's what friends are for," she said. "Remember, I'm only a call away."

I was feeling a bit lighter. "I'll keep that in mind. Take care of yourself, okay?"

"You too, Holli," she said. "Talk soon."

"Definitely," I said with a small smile, hanging up. A sense of relief washed over me. Knowing I had Samantha's support lifted my spirits, even if the road ahead with John was still uncertain.

I poured a glass of wine and sank onto the couch. I reached for a photo of John and I, taken during happier times. Holding it in my hands, I traced the contours of our smiles, remembering the joy we had once found in each other's company. Tears welled up in my eyes, a silent testament to the love that still lingered despite everything.

I made a quiet promise to myself. I wanted to cherish the memories we had created and honor the love we shared.

I sat there, staring at the half-empty glass of wine in my hand. It wasn't easy, but I recognized ending it with John was the right thing to do. The decision was made, and now I had to focus on moving forward, though my heart ached with the loss of what may have been.

Chapter 4

Reeling from my conversation with John the previous night, I woke up prepared to bury myself in legal briefs and contracts. On my way to the office, I grabbed coffee for Amanda and myself seemed like a good idea. I arrived at Smell of Brew.

I approached the counter. "I'd like two Americanos."

She nodded. "They'll be ready soon. Your name?"

"Holli."

The aroma of ground beans surrounded me inside. A soft acoustic guitar melody drifted from hidden speakers, complementing the gentle hum of patrons chatting over their morning brews. I settled at a weathered oak table, running my fingers along the smooth surface as I waited.

I called Amanda to check on the samples from the football field.

The phone rang twice. "Hello," she said.

"Hi."

"Hey, how are you?"

"I have been better. John and I broke up last night."

"What happened?"

I began to blink to hold back the tears. "We..." my voice faltered, words catching in my throat. "We argued about... about where we were headed." I blinked back tears, my fingers tightening around the mug.

"I am so sorry to hear that. It must suck," she said, trying to comfort me.

It hurts. Changing the subject, I said, "Listen, I'll be at the office soon. Do you have any news on the water samples?"

"Not yet. I'll put them on your desk when they arrive."

"Thanks. After analyzing them, we need to meet with the Titan executives."

"I'll set up the meeting."

"Okay"

I hung up and my mind drifted back to John. Was I putting ambition before family? I loved my job and had always aimed to become a partner, but the space between John and I was eating me inside.

"Holli?" the barista called.

I reached for my order, the aroma of roasted beans distracting me. A shadow fell over the table, and I witnessed a man with an outstretched hand.

"Holli?" He was calm, and his smile was genuine as he gave me a business card. I hesitated with his gaze with surprise and intrigue. "I overheard your call and thought I was able to help," he said, his voice steady and kind.

"Thank you," I said, glancing at the card. Jack Wright, Environmental Engineer. He had an air of quiet confidence, his casual attire contrasting with the seriousness of his offer.

Looking at him, I sensed a flicker of something – interest, curiosity, even attraction. I dismissed it, I desired to remain attentive to my lawsuit. The last thing I wanted was to jump from one relationship to another. It was unexpected and intriguing.

"I'd love to help," he said with a smile.

Blushing, I said, "I'll keep you in mind. I need to head off."

I got into the driver's seat, replaying the conversation. "You sounded like an idiot!" I scolded myself. He was handsome, but I knew I needed to stay focused. I sensed the urgency and was required to make it to the office and work on this situation.

I drove to the office. My thoughts drifted from John and the encounter with Jack. I parked and took a deep breath before stepping out. The city's hustle surrounded me, but my mind was still elsewhere.

Walking in, I handed Amanda her coffee. "Here you go," I said, forcing a smile that didn't quite reach my eyes.

She accepted the cup, her gaze lingering on me for a moment longer than usual. "Thanks, Holli," she said, her voice soft, almost cautious.

Her eyes searched mine, the slight furrow in her brow telling me she could sense something was off. She didn't say anything, but the unspoken understanding hung between us. Instead of pressing, she simply gave me a nod, offering silent support.

I stacked the files, labeled and prioritized them. I flipped open the top folder, pencil poised over the legal jargon. With each page turned, my focus sharpened and the outside world faded into the background.

A few hours later, Amanda knocked on my door. "The lab results are in," she said, handing me a file.

I opened it and scanned the pages. The contamination levels in the water were high. "I didn't expect this," I said.

"We need to schedule that appointment with Titan," she reminded me.

I looked at her. "Yes, let's do that. I met an environmental engineer this morning. He might be able to help us. Can you set up a time with him as well?"

She raised an eyebrow. "Sure, what's his name?"

"Jack Wright," I said, handing her his card.

She took it with a knowing smile. "I'm on it."

The day wore on, the buzz of excitement from the unfolding drama began to fade, replaced by thoughts of John that crept into the quiet moments. His smile, the way he'd always know how to make me laugh—it all lingered in the back of my mind, distracting me.

I caught myself thinking about our last conversation, wondering what could have been, but I shook my head, pushing the thoughts aside. *Not now*, I told myself. *This is your moment—focus on your career. That's what matters right now.* With a deep breath, I shifted my attention back to the tasks at hand.

Later that afternoon, Amanda came to my office and informed me that the Titan executives were unavailable.

"Can you please ask Titian if we can have a copy of their financials. We need to know what we can negotiate if it comes to a monetary settlement. Did you get a hold of Jack Wright?"

"Mr. Wright suggested we see him, after we met executives."

"Perfect," I said. "Thank you."

The office had emptied out hours ago, but I stayed behind, determined to review our strategy one more time. The evidence was solid—airtight, even—but I knew that wouldn't be enough. We had to present it flawlessly, with conviction, if we wanted to win. The weight of that responsibility kept me glued to my desk, pouring over the details, ensuring there were no gaps.

When I finally packed up, it was well past sunset. The city had settled into an unusual stillness, a far cry from the chaos of the day. The quiet felt like a relief as I stepped outside, but my mind refused to wind down.

As I made my way home, I found myself thinking about Jack again—his unexpected offer of help. There was something about it that I couldn't shake. It felt... timely, almost as if fate had stepped in.

I sighed, trying to let it go for the night, but the thought lingered, trailing behind me like a shadow.

My phone buzzed. It was my brother Steve. I needed to catch up with him and learn more about his move to Sunnyville.

I sunk into my sofa. "Hello,"

"Hey Holli, I can't wait to visit you and John."

I began to tear up. "It'll just be me. He and I broke up last night,"

"No way. I liked him."

"Life goes on. So, what's your news?"

"I'll work in the Bankruptcy department at Winston and Associates."

"That's fantastic! When do you start?"

Having him close by would be a welcome change. I missed our sibling bond; his support would mean the world to me with everything happening in my life.

I leaned back on the couch, the soft cushions surrounding me. The thought of him moving closer brought a flutter of relief. I closed my eyes, imagining family dinners and laughter echoing through the house, a balm to soothe the ache in my heart.

"They want me to begin later this month. Can I stay with you until Tiff and the kids move?"

"Of course. There's always room for you guys."

"They'll join on weekends. Tiffany's searching for houses."

"Got it. I'm looking forward to it!"

"Me too."

"Talk soon."

We hung up and I sunk deeper into the couch. Thinking about the day's events will help the healing process and what the future will hold.

I arrived at the office, exhausted. The conversation with Steve had given me a bit of a boost, but I recognized I had a long day ahead. The hum of conversations greeted me as I walked through the doors. It was comforting, almost grounding.

I made my way to my desk, passing colleagues who smiled. I returned their gestures, not up to any small talk. It had a mountain of files and documents on top. I took a deep breath and sat down, ready to immerse myself in work.

Amanda was already working, fingers dancing on the keyboard. We had been a team for so long that she could sense my mood. Her furrowed brow hinted that something was amiss. Without a word, she rose from her chair and headed towards my office.

"I've come across something intriguing regarding Titan," I said as she entered.

"Based on their latest quarterly balance sheet, they're facing challenges," she said, handing me a file.

I took the document from Amanda and scanned through it. The numbers painted a clear picture of financial instability within Titan. Their expenses escalated while their revenue stagnated, a precarious situation for any organization.

"This is quite telling," I said, looking into Amanda's eyes with a grin of appreciation. They're in a tight spot. Have they responded to our requests for an appointment?"

She shook her head. "Not yet. I've followed up twice since yesterday, but no response so far."

"Let's give them a bit more time," I folded the document and placed it on my desk. "In the meantime, we should prepare some strategic points. Highlight their financial vulnerabilities and how they relate any kind of settlement."

"I'll draft a report of the key ideas we want to emphasize. Should we plan for early next week?"

"Yes, that sounds reasonable," I leaned back in my chair and contemplated the future steps. "Let's aim for Tuesday morning. They'll have responded by then."

With a determined look, she returned to write the summary, leaving me to gather my thoughts. The challenge ahead was significant. I noticed a surge of energy, knowing we were on the correct track. We will uncover crucial details for our argument for Titan.

I dialed Justin's number, intent on updating him about the water findings and gathering any information he might have regarding the company.

"Hello?" Justin said, answering his phone.

"It's Holli. The testing results are in. Contamination levels are higher than anticipated. Arsenic exceeds safety limits."

"Can you forward the report to my attorneys?"

"Sure, I would be happy to but it won't look good for your position."

"I know. I just want to keep them in the loop. We trusted Titian because of their reputation. this will affect any further projects with them. It will also help us file a suit against TerraGuard for negligence."

"Ok Justin. Keep me in the loop as well and If I get any further information, I will let you know."

We hung up and I drumming my fingers on my desk. I needed to focus on sorting through the mounting files on my desk. I waited for Amanda to bring updates from the Titan executives. After a while, she appeared at the doorway.

"Good news," she said as she entered my office, her voice filled with anticipation. "I've scheduled an appointment with Titan for tomorrow afternoon."

Relief washed over me; I was grateful for Amanda. "That's excellent. Thank you for arranging this. We need to discuss the financials so we are ready to make a settlement."

"I'll make sure everything is prepared."

I smiled at her dedication. "Thanks. Can you also set up a time with Jack Wright? And can you find any different information out regarding the financials of Titan? I want to determine if they are hiding anything."

Amanda left with a determined smile, leaving me to gather my thoughts and preparations for tomorrow. The additional dialogue with Jack can provide valuable insights to help our argument. Just the idea made me blush and my heart raced.

Chapter 5

I sat at my desk. Piles of folders scattered across its surface. The early morning light filtered through the blinds, casting long shadows over the paperwork. The hum of conversations and ringing phones outside my office faded into the background. I stared at the files, my thoughts swirling around the intricacies of the case.

The water results ensured the lawsuit against Titan was straightforward. We will likely settle out of court with monetary damages. But something gnawed at me, an unsettling anxiety I couldn't shake.

I reclined back in my chair, eyes blurred as I tried to pinpoint my source of distress. It all seemed too easy. Titan had troubles and their quarterly balance sheets supported our claims. They had every reason to agree, avoiding further scrutiny. The pressure to settle quickly was coming from Davis, and I wondered why. Titian was in no position to financially settle but the rush to a resolution did not sit well with me.

I flipped through the lab reports again, scrutinizing the data. Did we missed something crucial in our haste?

A soft knock on the door pulled me from my thoughts. Amanda stepped in, her usual confident demeanor tempered by concern. "Holli, are you alright?"

"Yeah, just thinking. Something is off. It's almost too perfect, as if they're letting us witness what they want us to notice."

She tilted her head, considering my words. "Can you find out any different information regarding the financials of Titan?"

"Maybe," My mind was racing. "There's another layer we haven't uncovered yet. They're willing to settle, so it might be because they fear what would be found."

"You could be onto something. I know you will find it. Keep search." Amanda smiled at me and then left. I always appreciated the way how she would check up on me when things were busy. It was proof that we not only had a great working relationship but we genuinely cared about each other's well being. My thoughts drifted back to the case. I needed a person who could cut through my doubts and give me clarity. Someone like Denise, who had always seen through the fog when I couldn't. I picked up the phone and dialed. She would confirm my notion or direct me elsewhere. I picked up my phone and dialed her number. It only took one ring before someone answered.

"Hello?" came the familiar voice on the other end.

"Hi, It's Holli."

"It's so nice you called," she said. "How are you?"

"I've been better. I'm working on a matter, and something about it appears incorrect. The proof is solid, but it's too easy. I think we might be missing something important."

Denise's voice grew professional. "Tell me more."

I laid out the details for her. I discussed the arsenic levels in the water near the football field and Titan's economic troubles. I also told her about the strange ease with which they steer us toward an agreement.

"Holli," Denise said after a moment of silence. "I've learned over the years that you should always follow the evidence wherever it leads. Something is off. Trust your instincts. Don't rush into a deal because it's the easier path."

"I was worried you'd say that."

She chuckled. "I understand it's tempting to wrap things up when you have a strong case. Remember, your job is to seek the facts, not just win settlements. If there's more to this, uncover it. Review everything again. Explore Titan's practices and history further."

"Thank you," I said, "I needed to hear that."

"Anytime. Remember, I'm always here if you need to talk or receive advice. You're a brilliant lawyer and I have no doubt you'll reach the bottom of this."

We said our goodbyes and I hung up the phone. A sense of clarity washed over me. Denise was right, I couldn't let the allure of a quick deal distract me from my duty to uncover the fact. I had to follow the evidence, no matter where it led.

I called Amanda into my office, her eyes widening with curiosity as she sat down.

"We're going to investigate this," I said, my voice firm. "I want you to re-examine everything—Titan's history, financials, past projects. We need to find out what they're hiding."

"You got it."

I prepared for the meeting with Titan executives. This was a crucial moment in our case and I needed to be at my best. I had to be prepared for whatever might come our way.

My first task was to analyze the water testing findings again. The high arsenic levels were alarming, but I had to understand the implications. I pored over the data, making notes and highlighting key points. The numbers were damning, but I must present them irrefutably.

Amanda entered my office, holding a stack of files and placing them on my desk. "Here are the additional files you requested,"

"Thanks." I looked at her with an appreciative smile for her diligence. "I want to go over these. Let's make sure we have everything covered."

I spent the next few hours delving into the financial reports. The more I read, the more convinced I was that Titan was hiding something. Their financial troubles painted a picture of a company wanting to settle things quickly to not have further financial troubles.

Amanda and I went over our strategy. We outlined the key points we needed to address and anticipate the possible counterarguments. I wanted to ensure we were prepared for any curveballs Bill McAllister might throw our way.

Amanda looked up. "What happens if they deny everything?"

"We will have to explore more to find more proof so we can prove innocence or wrong doings." I hoped they would be forthright.

Amanda and I walked down the hallway. I took a deep breath and opened the door to the conference room. James McAllister, the CEO, was waiting and greeted us with a firm handshake and a confident smile. We took our seats.

"Thank you for gathering with us," I said. "I have concerns about your case. We do feel it is in your best interest to settle outside of court. It will help put the matter behind us and will help your reputation and your bottom line. However we have found some samples from an independent laboratory came back with high levels of arsenic."

He reclined back in his chair, arms crossed. "Our company operates with the highest integrity," he said, his tone unwavering. "We are committed to our projects being above reproach."

I nodded, determined to stay composed. "We have evidence suggesting your construction practices may have contributed to the matter."

McAllister's expression hardened. "That's not true. We have rigorous standards. Any pollution must be from another source."

Amanda looked at him, now speaking up. "We've reviewed your quarterly statements. They show signs of economic strain."

He shrugged. "Our finances are sound. I can provide records to prove it. This issue is not on us."

McAllister slid a folder across the table with glossy publications and fiscal documents. I skimmed through the papers, noting the polished presentation, but something still seemed off.

He continued, his voice firm. "You're looking for a culprit. Look at the analysis and at TerraGuard. They have documented proof of their responsibility to the contamination."

I glance at Amanda, who looked skeptical. "We will review these documents and follow up with TerraGuard," I said with finality.

McAllister had a smirk playing at the corners of his mouth with his arms crossed. "Do that. I'm confident you'll find we are not at fault. We are not the ones guilty of misconduct, and to be accused by our own attorney is unacceptable."

"We do need to follow facts, so we can prove your innocence to the city," I said.

The meeting ended and Amanda and I walked out, the weight of McAllister's denial heavy on our shoulders. Once outside the building, I turned to her. "This isn't adding up."

I knocked on Davis's office door, waiting his invitation to enter. Our firm's senior partner, Davis, commanded respect and authority, and I was always nervous when seeking his counsel.

"Come in," he said.

I entered, closing the door behind me and approached his desk. Davis looked up from his papers, his expression welcoming. The space was filled with legal books and framed diplomas, exuding an air of professionalism matching his demeanor.

"What can I do for you today Holli?"

I took a deep breath, steadying myself. "We met with Bill McAllister, and he denied everything and claimed their economic strength and integrity."

He relaxed his back in his chair, his demeanor thoughtful. "Titan is our client. We have to protect their interests above all else. Denials are standard in such cases."

"Something appears off," I persisted. "Their files looked solid, but McAllister's confidence was... too rehearsed. It's as if they're hiding something."

He sighed. "Holli, I understand your concerns, but we must tread carefully. Titan is a prominent entity, a prolonged legal battle may lead to a community backlash. We need to consider settling to avoid any upheaval."

I hesitated, absorbing his words. "Shouldn't we pursue the facts if they hide something?"

"Sometimes, the data is murky," Davis said. "Our priority is to protect our client. A settlement will mitigate risks and have a smoother resolution. Trust me, it's in everyone's best interest, including the community's."

I accepted his counsel. "I understand your point."

"Good," he said, his tone reassuring. "Let's focus on negotiating a favorable settlement. We'll ensure Titan emerges from this with minimal damage. Keep me updated on your progress."

With a sense of resignation, I thanked him and left his office. I was gripped by the complexities of our client's case versus the pursuit of justice. It was a delicate balance that would test my convictions as a lawyer.

I returned to my desk. The weight of the firm's loyalty to Titan pressed against my conscience, clashing with my resolve to uncover the truth. I desired a moment to gather my thoughts before diving back into work.

I dialed Justin's number, hoping to gain some perspective from a different angle. If anyone understood the ripple effects of Titan's actions it would be him.

The phone rang twice before he answered. "Hey Holli, what's up?" His voice carried a hint of concern, picking up on the seriousness of my tone.

"Justin, how is this case affecting the Youth Sports and Education Alliance?" I looked at the files on my desk.

He sighed. "Some of our donors are reconsidering their donations because of the association with Titan. They're worried about the integrity of our partnerships."

I frowned, sensing a pang of guilt. "I'm sorry to hear that. This whole situation is putting you in a bad spot."

"We rely on these donations to support so many kids. Losing their trust may set us back years."

"Have you thought about making a statement or addressing their concerns?"

"We've been discussing it," he said. "I'm torn. We need to be transparent. I don't want to make any conclusions before we realize the full extent of Titan's and the suit."

"That makes sense. It's a delicate balance between transparency and protecting your organization's interests."

"Yeah," he said again, his voice tinged with frustration. "I wish there was a clear answer."

I got up from my desk and went over to the window. "I understand. Just take it one step at a time. We will figure this out together."

"Thanks, Holli," he said.

"Be patient. We'll survive through this."

We hung up the phone. I began to rub my temples. Concern lingered in my mind. I pictured the disappointed faces of the kids at the Youth Sports and Education Alliance if donations dried up. The thought of letting them down chewed at my conscience. I could not let the stadium close and the fields not be in use. It mean too much to the community. I understood discussing it with Jack would provide a welcome distraction and new insights.

I reviewed the findings from Titan's supposed water sample tests. Doubts gnawed at me. Bill McAllister's insistence on their integrity and financial strength was rehearsed, and it was almost too convenient. I realized I wanted more than their records to challenge their claims. That's why discussing this case with Jack was crucial. He is an non-biased environmental engineer whose knowledge may clarify this case's murky waters. I punched in Jack's number and waited as the phone buzzed in my ear.

"Hello?"

"Hi, Jack. It's Holli. Do you have some time to go over the water findings at your office?"

"Sure. When were you thinking?"

"Would twenty minutes work?"

"I'll be here."

As I ended the call, a small smile crossed my face. I grabbed my keys from the desk. Heading out the door, I hoped this meeting would bring some much-needed clarity.

I couldn't deny the flutter of anticipation as I approached the building. Discussing the water sample findings with him and gaining his insights was needed.

It was in a modern, glass-fronted building on a bustling street corner in the city. The exterior boasted sleek lines and mirrored windows reflecting the skyline, giving it a contemporary and professional appearance. I parked my car and took a moment to collect my thoughts before entering.

The office was organized yet lived-in. It had a comfortable seating area for clients and a small coffee table with a few magazines and a potted plant.

As I entered, he greeted me with a warm smile. "What do you have for me today?" His voice was calm, and his demeanor reassuring.

"I've brought the results from Titan's water tests," I said, handing him the folder. "Here are the reports from our independent testing."

He adjusted his glasses. "Yes, I see that. They both paint quite a different picture."

I nodded, leaning forward. "The discrepancies are concerning. It's hard to ignore such contrasting consequences."

He flipped through the documents on his desk, pointing out specific data points. "The sampling locations are different. Bill's team focused on areas away from the football fields."

I furrowed my brow, tracing my finger over the maps. "Our samples were taken from near the fields. That's where it is most severe."

"Exactly. Sampling location is crucial. It affects what you find and how you interpret the findings."

I tapped my pen against the table, thinking aloud. "So, if their samples were misleading or selective..."

"... It may mean they're downplaying the issue," Jack finished my thought. "Worse, they might not be as diligent as they claim."

Jack crossed his arms. "It's a starting point. You'll need to explore. Consider another independent testing."

I smiled. "Thank you. Your expertise is invaluable."

He smiled. "Happy to help."

I let out a soft sigh. I wasn't any closer to discovering the reality and had more questions than answers. I put the car in drive and headed back to the office.

I decided to examine the latest files Amanda had compiled regarding Titan's financials and their purported proof of innocence. I pored over the papers, and my skepticism deepened. The figures aligned with their integrity and stability robustness narrative. It all appeared orchestrated, crafted to deflect blame and safeguard their reputation at any cost.

I let out a breath and began jotting down key discrepancies. The inconsistencies in Titan's financial reports called for a deeper look, every number demanding careful attention. The documents we received didn't match those McAllister had given us, and the differences were hard to ignore. Unsure who to trust, I reminded myself that Titan was our client. Still, I couldn't shake the feeling that Titian might have something to hide, but I'd needed to dig into TerraGuard and their involvement.

Rushing into a deal would be premature and compromise justice. The idea of conceding now is like a betrayal of my principles as a lawyer committed to seeking accountability.

Amanda's knock on my door interrupted my focused thoughts. She handed me a folder as she approached. "Holli, I've compiled everything you requested."

"Thank you." I scanned the financial records. "We need to analyze the reports."

She nodded in agreement. "I'll arrange it for tomorrow afternoon."

"What is your gut telling you?" I was gauging her instincts.

She paused, her expression thoughtful. "It tells me they're hiding something. I agree with you. These numbers appear too perfect, too arranged. It's like they're trying too hard to convince us."

I mirrored Amanda's concerns. "We can't afford to take their claims at face value. I want to verify if there's any factuality to Titan's accusations against them."

"Absolutely. I'll start digging further. There might be more to uncover."

I was at home savoring a dinner when a thought struck me. I would contact Samantha, someone with an uncanny knack for uncovering information. She had an effortless way of locating details on anyone. After finishing, I moved to my patio. The night was beautiful, offering a stunning view of the sun descending over the ocean. I soaked in the scene. The phone began to ring.

"Holli! It's been ages. How are you?"

"Hey, Sam! I'm swamped with work, as usual. How's life treating you?" I reclined back in my chair and gazed at the water.

"I'm always juggling a million things. I took a little vacation last month. Went to Italy. It was amazing," Samantha said, her voice filled with the joy of recent memories.

"That sounds incredible. I've always wanted to go. I'm glad you took time for yourself and Seth," I said.

"What's up? I can tell there's something on your mind,"

I laughed while taking off my shoes while holding my phone to my ear. "You always read me like a book. Can I have your assistance? I'm looking into a company called Titian Construction, whose CEO is Bill McAllister. I need any information I can on them. You're the best at this sort of thing."

"Bill McAllister, huh? Sounds like a task for my magic touch," Samantha said. "Give me a couple of days."

"Thanks, Sam." I said. "You can email whatever you find to my paralegal, Amanda. You should still have her email address. She'll handle it from there."

"Got it. Amanda's the one with the glasses and the serious resting face, right?" she joked.

I laughed. "That's the one. You're amazing, Sam. I don't understand how you always pull these things off."

"It's a gift," she said with mock seriousness. "I'm happy to help. Anything for you."

"You're a lifesaver, Sam," I said, my voice softening. "I miss you. We need to catch up."

"Let's not let so much time pass next time. Take care, Holli,"

"You too, Sam. Talk soon," I said, experiencing a pang of nostalgia. I smiled, knowing that Samantha was on the case and I was in fantastic hands.

Chapter 6

O ver the next few days, I worked in my office on various cases demanding my attention. The morning sunlight filtered through the blinds, casting a gentle pattern on the stacks of files and legal texts that crowded my desk. Every dispute required meticulous mediation and negotiation, which I undertook with unwavering focus. The hum of computers and the distant chatter of colleagues in adjacent offices provided a steady backdrop to my efforts.

Client meetings filled my mornings. Each person brought unique concerns, which I listened to and noted down details. My afternoons were spent drafting documents. Agreements, motions, and letters flowed from my pen. I reviewed every word, ensuring accuracy.

Some cases require more creativity. I brainstormed solutions, thinking outside the box. It was satisfying to view progress.

Amanda walked into my office, holding a stack of records. "Samantha emailed me," she said, with surprise and relief. "Where did she discover this? I've been searching for days."

I smiled. "That's one of Samantha's secrets – if she tells you that, she'd have to shoot you."

We laughed, breaking the tension. This light moment was a rare respite from the constant pressure. I often wondered how I managed to stay afloat amidst the chaos. Moments like these kept me going.

Amanda handed me the papers and I scanned through the pages. "This is incredible. She came through."

She leaned in. "What did she find?"

I pointed to a highlighted section. "Samantha uncovered some crucial information. McAllister made payments to an offshore account in the Cayman Islands. It was a large sum of money."

Amanda's eyes widened. "Wow. That's significant." She held up another document.

"More exists. She also unearthed that Titan filed for Bankruptcy Protection under Chapter 11."

She gasped. "Bankruptcy? That's unexpected."

"Yeah, it changes the whole picture. Here's an email from McAllister to an unknown recipient. It reads, 'We can leave it alone for now. It passed the test, and I can use these results if anything comes up. It's a matter of time until we seal our reputation.'"

Amanda sat on the corner of my desk. "It sounds like he's covering tracks. What's our next move?" She was getting ready to leave.

I looked at the papers on my desk. "We analyze everything. Let's ensure we have a comprehensive understanding before deciding our strategy."

"I'll start working on it right away."

"Thank you."

With that, she left me to delve deeper into the wealth of information Samantha had unearthed. This may be the breakthrough for the case. I rubbed my temples, the information settling in. Samantha's findings suggested we were representing a guilty party—one I was supposed to settle with and let slip under the radar.

I needed insights from trusted sources required speaking with construction manager Joseph Flanigan, which is crucial for details on sample locations and times. He was the Project Manager for Titian Construction and over the years became a good friend. Picking up the phone I dialed Joe's number.

"Hi Joe, it's Holli Bauchman. Can I meet later to discuss the Youth Sports and Education Alliance football fields?"

"Sure. I'm always available for you."

"Thanks. I'll be there this afternoon."

"Okay, I'll be here," he said.

"Goodbye," I ended the call.

I considered inviting Jack along. His expertise remained undeniable. I wanted to invite him myself. I took the phone and sat on the couch in my office.

"Hey, it's Holli Bauchman. I was hoping we might talk about something important."

"Of course. What's on your mind?" he said, his tone friendly.

I got up and looked out the window "I plan to meet with Joe Flanigan later. Would you be available to join me?"

There was a brief pause, and he said, "I can make time for that."

"Thanks. I'll swing by your office before heading over." I was relieved that he could come along.

"Looking forward to it."

We arrived at Joe's, greeted by his welcoming smile as we entered. The space was tidy, with blueprints and schedules on his desk. Joe gestured us to take a seat as he closed the door behind us.

"Welcome," he said.

I jumped in, eager to reach the heart of the matter. "We're here to discuss the football stadium project. We need to go over the water analysis process."

He pulled out a folder. "We took samples from various points across the grounds last month. I can show you the locations on the site map."

He laid out the details, and Jack and I exchanged glances, taking mental notes.

"Can you take us where and when they were taken?" I said, eager to delve into specifics.

Jack leaned forward, studying the map. "What depths did you sample at?"

"At varying depths, from surface level down to one meter," Joe pointed to different spots. "This allowed us to assess quality throughout."

Jack nodded, impressed. "The timing of the sampling sessions?"

"We started early in the morning before any activities began on the fields," Joe said. "It ensured minimal disruption and accurate results."

I peeked at Jack, acknowledging his expertise in these matters. "What about the testing process?"

"We sent them to a certified lab specializing in soil analysis," Joe said. "They followed strict protocols to maintain accuracy."

We asked more technical questions about equipment calibration and contamination prevention. Joe responded with detailed explanations, demonstrating his team's meticulous approach.

I thanked him for the comprehensive overview. "This gives us a solid foundation to assess the suitability for the football fields."

Jack shook his hand. "Thanks, Joe. Your insights are invaluable."

"I'm glad to help. If you need anything else, call me."

We left Joe's office. The crisp air outside was a welcome change from the stuffy conference room. "Joe's confident in the process," I said, breaking the silence. "I think we have complete data to move forward."

Jack nodded. "Agreed. His explanations were thorough. It's clear they've taken all necessary precautions."

We began to drive back to Jack's office. He looked at me and shifted the conversation. "How's everything going at your end? Any new cases keeping you on your toes?"

I chuckled, the sound lightening the mood. "Always. We've got a few interesting clients coming in next week. One of them is a big merger case...should be challenging."

He smiled. "Sounds intense, how do you manage to juggle all these high-stakes cases?"

I shrugged. "Well, you get accustomed to the pressure. It helps to have a capable team. How about you? How are things on your side?"

He sighed. "Busy, as usual. I enjoy it, keeps me sharp." We continued chatting, the conversation flowing. "Have you had any time to relax or do something fun?"

I laughed. "Not as much as I'd like, though I was able to get away for a weekend. It was good to unplug for a bit."

"I've been meaning to take some time off, too. A short trip somewhere quiet."

We approached his office and he paused, turning to face me. "Holli, would you like to grab coffee sometime?"

I smiled, appreciating the gesture. It had been so long since I had taken time for something as simple as a casual coffee. The idea was both appealing and intimidating. "I'd like that."

"Perfect," he said, opening the door and entering his office. "I will give you a call sometime."

I drove back to Winston and Associates. I couldn't help but feel a flutter of excitement.

I sat alone at my desk, nestled in the cozy corner. Around me, shelves lined with legal texts and mementos created a comforting backdrop. The surface was cluttered with files and a half-finished cup of coffee. Outside the window, the afternoon sun painted long shadows across the bustling city streets below. It contrasted with the quiet reflection filling my mind after my conversation with Jack.

The meeting with Joe had gone well and Jack's invitation had left me joyful and lighthearted. It was rare to find such ease during our demanding work. I anticipated it would be a chance to build a connection beyond our professional interactions.

I didn't spot Amanda entering the room until she was right before me with a look and a stack of documents.

"Holli, you'll want to view this," she said, placing the papers on my desk. "Samantha sent over more crucial files."

She passed me a paper. "We also have an email from McAllister. He tells of an unknown recipient who lives in the Caymans."

My heart raced as I read McAllister's note. "This is clear proof of misconduct. They're hiding money offshore."

Her eyes were wide open. "We've got a name, a whistleblower from inside Titian."

I looked up, astonished. "A whistleblower? This might be the breakthrough we anticipated."

"Yes. They're ready to speak out about the company's practices."

I sensed a surge of determination. "This information will expose all the misconduct."

"I'll start preparing a detailed review."

I examined the filing, and a thought formed: "Please dig deeper. We have to understand every detail and angle. There might be more to uncover."

Amanda nodded. "We need to realize if this is a tactic to divert attention or a genuine economic issue."

I replied. "Check for any inconsistencies or red flags that may point to further misconduct."

She made a note in her planner. "I'll start with the financial records and look for hidden assets or unusual transactions."

"Perfect. This might be the key to bringing everything to light."

I glanced at the documents again. The case had just taken a dramatic turn.

She smiled. "We've got this."

I called after her. "You are doing a wonderful job!"

With a final nod of assurance, she exited, leaving a faint scent of her floral perfume lingering in the air. I took a deep breath, steeling myself to dive into the stack of files she had placed on my desk.

My phone rang as I was about to focus on the new information. Justin's name flashed on the screen.

"Hey, Justin," I sounded upbeat despite the day's weight.

"I have some bad news," he said, his voice tense. "TerraGuard just filed a defamation lawsuit against Titan and the Youth Sports and Education Alliance."

A cold knot formed in my stomach. "What? On what grounds?"

"They're arguing that our public statements about the contamination were defamatory and caused financial damage to their company,"

I rubbed my temples. "This is exactly what we didn't need."

"There's more. I've got some personal issues going on as well."

I paused, concerned. "What's happening?"

Justin sighed. "Brittany and I are having problems."

"I'm sorry to hear that," I said. "Is there anything I can do to help?"

"Just keep me in the loop with everything."

"Of course. We're in this together. The firm will handle the lawsuit and the contamination issue."

"Thanks, I appreciate it," he said, his voice softening. "I'll update you on my end, too."

"Take care. We'll get through this."

I hung up the phone. The lawsuit from TerraGuard was a threat, and Justin's struggles added another layer of complexity. I needed to be ready for the challenges.

Amanda re-entered the room just as I finished the call. "Holli, everything okay?"

"No, it's not." I looked at her and informed her about the filing. "I need to talk with Davis and obtain his opinion on where we go from here."

I made my way to Davis's office, my thoughts racing. The fluorescent lights cast a harsh glow on the polished floors. I might detect a faint hum of conversations from other offices, a stark contrast to the whirlwind of ideas in my mind. I passed the break room, catching a whiff of coffee, but it did nothing to calm my nerves.

His door loomed ahead, a symbol of authority and decision-making. I paused for a moment, before knocking.

"Come in," came the familiar, authoritative voice.

I opened the door and stepped inside. He sat behind his massive oak desk, gazing at a stack of papers. He glanced up as I entered, his expression unreadable.

"Holli, take a seat," he said, gesturing to the chair opposite him.

I sat down, clutching the proof. "We have some new developments. I need to discuss them with you."

He leaned back, entwining his fingers. "Go ahead."

I opened the folder and spread the paper on his desk. "We've received information, including a whistleblower's statement, a chapter 11 filing for Titian Construction and an email from McAllister indicating they're hiding money offshore. This is bigger than we thought."

He looked at the records before looking back at me. "And?"

"This evidence points to significant misconduct. McAllister is involved in financial deceit and the testimony may reveal everything. We can't ignore this."

He sighed, rubbing his temples. "Holli, I understand your concerns, but we need to be pragmatic. This matter is drawing too much attention and becoming a PR nightmare."

I frowned, I couldn't believe what I was hearing. "We might uncover the full extent of their wrongdoing."

He shook his head. "Sometimes, the best course of action is to settle. It will make this all disappear. The more this drags on, the more it jeopardizes our client's reputation and resources."

I sensed frustration rising within me. "Settling means we're letting them get away with it. This proof is solid."

"Holli," he said, his tone firm. "It is the safest option. We can negotiate terms that protect our interests and end this. The evidence you've gathered is significant, but it also poses a risk. We go to court, the outcome is not guaranteed."

I sat back, his words sinking in. "So, you want us to settle?"

"Yes," he said. "Prepare a settlement proposal. Let's resolve this without further escalation."

"I'll initiate it."

"Good," he said. "You've done excellent work, Holli. Sometimes, the best victories are the ones that never make it to the battlefield."

I stood up, gathering the papers. "Thank you."

I left his office and returned to mine. I sat in my chair and let out a sigh. I couldn't shake the notion that an opportunity for justice might slip by. The proof was clear and significant, yet the directive to prepare for a settlement was straightforward. Balancing practicality with the urge to pursue justice, I pondered the implications of my chosen path.

Uncertainty loomed over the following steps, with potential risks ahead. Amidst these considerations, one thing remained steadfast—my commitment to uncovering the truth, even if it meant reevaluating our approach. Stepping into my office, I recognized this moment as pivotal, one that could impact not only this case, but also my professional journey.

Chapter 7

Morning came with a soft golden glow filtering through the window blinds, casting warm hues across my desk. The hum of city traffic and the gentle chirping of birds outside created a serene backdrop to my thoughts. Davis's directive echoed in my mind. It was cautious, aiming for a swift resolution.

The proof we found—the offshore dealings, the whistleblower, and murky finances—revealed deceit. This impacts Youth Sports and Education Alliance, a charity I care about.

Clarity was elusive. Lawsuit risks the client's reputation, and settlements might overlook revelations. Seeking guidance, I called Denise. Her wisdom steered me through uncertainty, and I needed her legal, ethical, and strategic views.

Dialing her number, the knot of tension in my stomach eased with each ring. After a few chimes, she picked up, her warm voice calming my nerves.

"Hello, Holli. How are you?" Denise's familiar tone carried a sense of reassurance.

"Hi. I've...to make a difficult decision. I have significant proof, but Davis is leaning towards settling."

There was a brief pause, I could almost sense her processing the data. "Tell me more about this evidence," she prompted.

I launched into the details, the suspicious transactions, and the implications of Titian Construction filing bankruptcy. I pointed out that there was a whistleblower who would speak to the allegations of misconduct. She listened, interjecting with probing questions that helped me articulate my concerns.

"It sounds like you're at a crossroads," Denise said. "Balancing ethical and integrity imperatives with pragmatic considerations is never easy."

"I understand. I can't shake the impression that settling would be a missed opportunity to uncover the truth."

Denise's response was measured, yet supportive: "Trust your instincts. You've always had a knack for seeing beyond the surface. Sometimes, the untrodden path yields the greatest rewards."

Her words resonated with me. "Thank you."

"Anytime. Keep me updated on how things progress," she said.

I hung up, feeling somewhat reassured but still conflicted. Amanda entered my office with a young attorney.

"Good morning! This is Michelle Zimmerman. She was just assigned to our team by Davis to work on the Titian Construction case."

I extended a welcoming hand to her. "Nice to meet you. Welcome aboard."

I noticed Michelle's posture straighten as she looked around the office, her eyes briefly sweeping over the case files stacked neatly on the desks and the awards displayed on the walls. She smiled, clearly eager to make a positive impression.

"Thank you," she said, her voice steady but enthusiastic. "I've learned a lot about the challenging cases you handle here. I'm excited to contribute."

Amanda caught my eye, indicating that we should continue our discussion from earlier. "Can you please give us a moment?"

"Of course," she said, stepping back. I'll catch up on some reading in my office."

When she left, Amanda turned back to me. "So, how did it go with Denise?"

I sighed, leaning back in my chair. "She was supportive, as always."

Amanda went and sat on the sofa in my office. "It's not an easy spot to be in. What's your gut telling you?"

"I understand the risks of dragging this out and the damage it could bring to Titian financially and their reputation."

"I've been digging deeper into the finances of Titian Construction since we got those files. Something is going on. The bankruptcy filing might not be as straightforward."

"That worries me too. If we settle now, we might never uncover the full extent of their misconduct."

"We could request more time to investigate," Amanda suggested. "Buy us some breathing room to validate the whistleblower's claims and gather more information

I considered Amanda's proposal, seeing a potential middle ground. "That might be our best move right now. Let's prepare a plan for Davis. We might have a chance if we can convince him that delaying the settlement will strengthen our position."

She began to leave. "I'll start drafting a strategy outline. We'll need to present a compelling argument."

"Thanks,"

There was something else on my mind, too—the arrival of Michelle Zimmerman. Why had he now assigned her to our team in such a critical phase?

I couldn't shake the sensation that her timing wasn't coincidental. Was she here to support our efforts, or was another agenda at play? Davis's decisions were always calculated, and her background in corporate law hinted at a strategic move.

Resolving to give her responsibilities and involve her in our strategy discussions, I also realized I needed to watch her. Her fresh perspective could be invaluable, but trust had to be earned in this sensitive matter. I would keep an eye on how she handled herself. Every detail mattered, now more than ever, and her presence may tip the scales in ways I've not yet anticipated.

I walked down to her office and gently knocked on her door.

"Good morning," she said, her tone polite.

"Morning," I replied, as i walked in the door and sat across from her. "I wanted to personally welcome you to the team. It's an essential time for us."

Her expression attentive. "Thank you, Holli. I'm eager to contribute in any way I can."

I hesitated in choosing my words. "I'm curious, though. What prompted Davis to assign you now, given your background in corporate law?"

Michelle's smile widened with a glint of professionalism. "I believe it's because of my experience with complex economic structures and negotiations. I can offer insights into strategic planning and risk management in defemination cases."

I sensed there was more beneath the surface. "How do you feel about being involved in a matter like this, with the recent developments?"

She replied calmly, her posture composed, "It's a tough situation, but I'm prepared to handle it. I really want to help the team succeed."

That was a thoughtful response, indeed, but I had to be cautious. "I understood that we need to focus on ethics and integrity."

She didn't waver in her professionalism. "I appreciate your honesty, and I'm dedicated to maintaining the highest standards."

I sat down in one of the chairs in her office and began by updating her on the latest developments in the case. I outlined the key points—McAllister's offshore dealings, water samples, the whistleblower's identification, and the discrepancies in the fiscal records of Titian Construction. She listened, showing she was following along.

After I finished, Michelle leaned forward. "I understand the overview, but I'm curious about the specifics of the monetary notes Amanda mentioned. Do you have copies?"

"Not yet. She assured me she'd have them ready."

She looked at the documents. "I'd like to review them to understand the economic irregularities better. It may help us strategize our approach."

I agreed with her assessment. "I'll ensure you have access as soon as possible."

"What about the whistleblower? Do we have facts about him? Have we spoken with him?"

Shaking my head. "Not yet. I think it's time we visited him. He can provide invaluable insights into what's happening at Titian Construction."

I got up to leave. "It's important to hear from the whistleblower and understand his motivations. It might also let us know how credible his claims are."

"Let's see him together. I'll coordinate with Amanda to set it up. The sooner we gather more data, the better prepared we'll be."

"Perfect," she said with a smile. "Thanks for trusting me as a new team member. Not many would be as gracious nor want someone this late."

"I am not like everyone you meet here." I winked at her and left for my office.

We drove from Winston & Associates to a corner bar. The streets outside were bustling with midday activity. The neon sign flickered, casting over the worn wooden tables and hushed conversations. The scent of aged oak and faint traces of cigar smoke lingered in the air, adding to the stealthy atmosphere.

I glanced at Michelle as she reviewed our prepared notes. "Do you have everything you need?"

"I think so. We've got the key questions mapped out. Let's hope he's forthcoming."

My mind raced through the potential outcomes of this meeting. "Remember, his name is Mike Stevens. He used to work in the finance department at Titian Construction."

We parked and made our way into the lit bar. I spotted a man sitting in a corner booth. His weary demeanor matched the gravity of the situation. "Mr. Stevens?" I approached.

He looked up. "Yes, that's me. You must be Holli," he said, extending his hand.

I shook his hand. "This is my colleague Michelle," I said, gesturing to her, and smiled.

"Nice to meet you," Michelle said "Thank you for agreeing to meet with us."

He nodded, his eyes darting around as if assessing the level of privacy. "No problem. I've been waiting for someone to listen."

We settled into the booth, ordering drinks to ease the tension. Soon enough, her tone was gentle yet probing. "Can you tell us more about what you uncovered at Titian Construction?"

He sighed, running a hand through his hair. "It's a mess. The finances are all over the place. There are shell companies, inflated invoices, and money being siphoned off. It's like they were bleeding the company dry."

"Can you give us specifics? How were they hiding the transactions?"

My eyes narrowed. "Did you have access to these records?"

Mike hesitated. "Yes, I kept copies. I realized something wasn't right, and I wanted proof."

"Where are they now? Can we examine them?"

He looks around the bar. "I... I didn't bring them, but I can obtain them for you. Give me a few days."

I exchanged glances with Michelle, agreeing that this would be promising information. "That would be helpful, Mike. We appreciate your willingness to share this with us."

We continued to delve into the details of the fraudulent activities. Michelle took the lead in probing deeper into the intricacies, asking pointed questions that uncovered more layers of deceit. Her methodical and precise approach guided Mike through the labyrinth of fraudulent transactions and misleading financial records.

Mike's relief was profound. The gravity of his revelations became increasingly unmistakable as we pieced together the evidence. Mike's anxiety transformed into cautious optimism as he realized that his whistleblowing was being heard and acted upon with the seriousness it deserved.

Leaving the bar, we walked to the car in silence. Mike's attestation made the corruption in Titian Construction clearer. I could watch the gears turning in Michelle's mind.

"We need to verify everything," I said, starting the engine. "This evidence may be pivotal."

Michelle nodded. "Agreed. This changes things. We must act fast before they can cover their tracks."

I was shocked. My surprise was notice. We exchanged glances. We discussed our next steps, outlining how we would cross-reference Mike's details with the documents we already had.

I arrived at Winston and Associates, Michelle, Amanda and I went to my office, closed the door behind us, and I turned to Michelle. "There's something else we need to consider, my brother Steve, will soon be working here. He specializes in bankruptcy and has a sharp eye. I think he might be a valuable asset."

She looked intrigued. "Does he have experience with this kind of investigation?"

"Yes, he's worked on a few cases involving fraud. I trust his judgment. He might detect something we've missed."

I picked up the phone and called him. After a few rings, he answered. "What's up?"

"We've got some new facts from a whistleblower that can be crucial," I said. "Can you help us investigate the financials and verify his claims?"

There was a pause as he absorbed the knowledge. "I can come in the morning. I'll review the files related to the bankruptcy and explore what I can find."

"Thanks."

"Understood. I'll catch up with you both."

Amanda stared at us. "That sounds like a solid plan. I should also mention that Bill McAllister has requested a meeting to receive an update on the matter."

I perceived a surge of urgency. "Can we schedule that for tomorrow afternoon? We need time to review and discuss everything with Steve."

"I'll set it up," Amanda said. "Make sure to cover all bases beforehand. McAllister will want comprehensive answers."

"Thanks," I said. "We'll be ready."

She left my office, and I turned to Michelle. "We have some time."

She stood up and moved towards the door. "I will begin working on it."

I watched her leave, and my mind was already going. My phone buzzed. Glancing at the screen, I spotted a message from Jack:

"Hey, just checking in. Can we catch up over coffee?"

A smile crept across my face as I typed back, "Tomorrow after 6 PM works for me!"

I set it aside and couldn't help but think of him. The thought of coffee together left me with a sense of warmth and anticipation.

Refocusing on the tasks, I began preparing for tomorrow. I dedicated the evening to a thorough review of the case material, and reviewed the evidence and legal documents, ensuring every detail was accounted for and ready to be presented. My discussions earlier with Michelle and Steve were invaluable as we brainstormed strategies and developed a cohesive plan to tackle the next steps in the case. Their expertise and perspectives added insight crucial in addressing the complexities.

As the night grew late, the dim light of my desk lamp shown over the papers and notes scattered before me. Despite my exhaustion, I knew tomorrow would be pivotal, and I needed it to be at my best. I wrapped up my preparations with a clear focus, knowing that our strategies' success and the case's integrity relied heavily on our collective efforts.

I finally decided it was time to leave the office. Arriving home, I allowed myself a brief time to unwind. I knew a good night's sleep was essential for the demanding day ahead, so I aimed to embrace it fully.

Chapter 8

I merged onto the freeway, and to sing to the familiar song that was playing. My phone buzzed with Amanda's name on the screen. I tapped the answer button, and the Bluetooth connected seamlessly to my car's audio system.

"Morning," her voice came through the speakers, clear despite the rush of passing cars. "I left the updated files in your office. They should give us a clearer picture for today."

"Thanks, Amanda," I said, grateful for her efficiency. "I'll review them as soon as I get in."

We exchanged a few more words about our strategy for the upcoming meeting with Bill McAllister. Her calm demeanor was reassuring and her insights were always valuable. I drove through the last turns toward the building as we concluded the call.

The office was quiet at this hour; the only sound was the early birds beginning to trickle in. I found the folder Amanda had mentioned on my desk. I opened it and looked over its contents.

The numbers and charts told a story of economic irregularities and questionable transactions within Titian Construction. Each page brought new insights and raised fresh questions. I scribbled notes in the margins, marking key points and connecting dots as I worked through the specifics.

Time slipped away as I delved deeper into the records, absorbing the implications of the discovery. The proof was compelling, depicting wrongdoing that demanded our attention. I reviewed, my focus sharpened, and my determination to uncover the truth grew stronger every minute.

Immersing myself in the files, the office came to life around me. The quiet hum of early activity filled the air as colleagues exchanged greetings and settled into their routines. Steve entered amidst this backdrop, his brisk steps announcing his arrival.

"Morning, Holli," His eyes scanned the papers in my hand. "I understand we've got some interesting discoveries from the whistleblower."

I handed him the folder and he took it with a nod of thanks... "It's quite a trove. Amanda compiled everything we've gathered so far."

He flipped through the pages, pausing briefly to jot down notes or furrow his brow in concentration. His experience with fiscal fraud cases made him an asset, so I trusted his insights.

"Looks like we've got some digging to do," he said, his expression thoughtful.

"Yeah, the deeper we go, the more it unravels," My voice reflected the gravity of our conclusions.

He. "I'll cross-reference these with the bankruptcy filings and determine if anything jumps out. Keep me posted on any new developments."

"Will do," I smiled at him, appreciating his proactive approach.

He left my office, his mind already churning to the task. He disappeared down the hallway, knowing his meticulous scrutiny would uncover facts.

There was a light knock and Michelle stepped in, her expression determined yet eager. "Morning, Holli."

"Good morning," I smiled at her energy. "I have the files Amanda mentioned. They're right here," I said, gesturing toward the stack of papers on my desk. "They should give us more information about the economic aspects we discussed yesterday."

Her gaze flicking between the papers and me. "Thanks, I'll dive into these."

"Steve is down the hall on the left. He's been going through some of the information, too. You might want to sync up with him."

"Will do," Michelle said with a nod, already starting to leaf through the papers. "I'll let you know if I find anything significant."

With that, she walked out, her footsteps echoing down the hallway. I returned to my tasks and I couldn't help but feel reassured by Michelle's diligence and focus.

Focusing on the upcoming meeting with McAllister, I aimed to withhold certain things while remaining open to his input.

Amidst my preparations, Amanda's message came through:

"Holli, McAllister's assistant, called. He's requesting an earlier time than scheduled."

Glancing at the clock, I realized time was slipping away faster than expected.

"When?" I said.

"In an hour. I've summarized the key discoveries and highlighted the discrepancies and variations. This should help guide our discussion."

I bit my lip in contemplation before typing back:

"Thanks, Amanda."

I rose from my seat and hurried to Steve's office with the news. "We have a change of plans. The meeting is in an hour."

Steve and Michelle gathered around the table, ready to strategize. "Did you find anything significant?" Steve asked as he approached me.

"Yes," he said. " Everything the whistleblower stated is in those files. There was proof of inflated invoices, evidence of embezzlement—funds siphoned off to shell companies."

Michelle chimed in, confirming their results. "We verified money was sent to the Cayman Islands."

"What about the bankruptcy filing?" I pressed further.

He rubbed his temples. "I'm not sure about that one. The paperwork appears to be in order and filed, but something about it is suspicious."

We left Steve's office, the urgency of our purpose palpable. Michelle walked beside me, her heels clicking on the polished marble floors. Steve followed behind, carrying a stack of key-organized papers.

The pressure was intense as we entered in the conference room. We waited for McAllister to arrive. McAllister entered, and his demeanor was as expected—confident, bordering on arrogant.

"Ah, Ms. Bachman," McAllister said with a smirk. "I am glad you were able to meet with us today."

I gestured for everyone to sit, trying to keep my cool despite his dismissive tone. "Mr. McAllister, we are here to update you on the situation with Titian Construction's legal issues. We believe that we can negotiate and settle the water contamination issue. It will cost some money, so we delved into the company's fiscal picture."

Taking a breath, I glanced at Steve and Michelle, "We've uncovered several inconsistencies in the documents related to our financial review. We need to discuss these irregularities with you."

He leaned back in his chair, his smirk widening. "I don't know what you are talking about. I have already shared with you, our company is fiscally solid."

Michelle jumped in, her voice steady. "We do have inconsistences within your balance sheet."

McAllister's facade faltered, replaced by a hint of defensiveness. "I have already shared with Ms. Bauchman our current financials. That's standard business practice. Your team lacks understanding of how business transactions work."

Steve, who had been reviewing reports, spoke up. "Mr. McAllister, we're here to lay the foundation of a settlement for your case. The inconsistencies must be resolved for us to move forward. We won't hesitate to escalate our conclusions if necessary."

McAllister chuckled dismissively. "Ms. Bauchman, I think you're overstepping here." He leaned forward, his eyes narrowing. "What does this have to do with water contamination?"

"Is that all you have for me?" he said.

Exchanging a knowing glance with Michelle and Steve, I noted his defensive reactions. We left the conference room. His smirk lingered in my mind, accompanied by a growing suspicion.

I moved towards the door. "Yes. We will contact you with all the information."

"Perfect. I will wait to hear from you and we can put this all behind us." He walked out and headed to the elevator. McAllister stepped in and the elevator doors closed.

"He is hiding something," I said aloud.

"He sure is a piece of work. I'd love to have 20 friends just like him," Steve said.

"His company is going to pot, and he's acting like he doesn't care," I said. I needed to inform Davis about the results of the discussion and our plans to negotiate with the plaintiff. We still had to investigate the company's economic well-being.

Leaving the conference room, my mind buzzed with questions. I needed to talk to Davis. The hallway stretched ahead, long and quiet, the walls lined with framed certificates and photos. Each step echoed, a reminder of the gravity of our situation.

At Davis's office, I knocked and waited for his response. His voice called out, inviting me in. I opened the door and stepped inside.

"Holli, what brings you here?" He asked, setting aside a stack of papers.

"I just had a meeting with McAllister to set up the financial for the settlement. His reactions were...unsettling. He denied everything, but there was something off about how he did it."

Davis leaned back in his chair, steepling his fingers. "Bill is protecting himself."

"I understand that, but he was too defensive. Almost like he was hiding something," I said, hoping he'd realize the urgency.

He sighed, rubbing his temple. "We've been through this. Sometimes pushing too hard can backfire." Mr. Davis's gaze hardened. "Settlements are often the most practical solution. Dragging this out prolongs harm to everyone involved, including us."

I hesitated for only a moment before continuing to push. "We can uncover more with a deeper inquiry."

He looked at me, his expression thoughtful. "McAllister and I go back. We don't want to destroy reputations."

Walking toward the door, I said, "I understand, Mr. Davis, but any wrongdoing needs to be addressed."

"Settle the case, and let's move on."

"I'll keep you updated."

Leaving Davis's office, my mind raced with questions and suspicions. I needed to talk to Steve and Michelle about what happened.

"We must be careful," I said, joining them.

Steve was surprised. "What's going on?"

"He is steadfast on settling, and I now have a hunch needing confirmation."

He raised an eyebrow. "Do you think he's covering for McAllister?"

"I don't know. We can't trust everyone."

She was uneasy. "What do you mean?"

"Keep your eyes open," I said. "There are too many coincidences. Be cautious with who you share information with."

Sitting at my desk, I replayed my conversation with Davis. "I almost missed it. It is all beginning to make sense. I need to receive confirmation..." I said to myself.

My phone buzzed, the sudden vibration interrupting my silence. A smile spread across my face as I picked it up. It was Jack. His message was simple:

"How is it going? I can't wait until we have coffee. When are you available?"

Thinking for a moment, I quickly began to type, and hit send.

"I can meet tomorrow morning. How about at The Smell of Brew at 7:30?"

Almost immediately, a response came through.

"See you then."

I bit my upper lip and smiled. I called Steve's office. "Are you ready to go to the house?"

"Sure thing. Let me collect my things."

I met Steve in the hallway. We took the elevator down together, the quiet ding announcing each floor. The warm evening breeze greeted us as we made our way to our cars and drove through the familiar streets of Sunnyville.

At my house, the atmosphere shifted to a more relaxed mood. We settled in, the sound of clinking pots and pans filling the kitchen as we cooked spaghetti and poured glasses of wine. Soon, the rich, inviting aromas of garlic bread and simmering sauce filled the room.

Sitting down, I peered at Steve. "I have my hunch about what's going on, but I want confirmation before I take action."

"Who are you going to ask for help?"

"Do you remember Denise?"

"I do," he said. "She is brilliant!"

"She will need to look at some things and contact Samantha."

He glanced at me. "Ah, your secret weapon!"

"Yes! She has come up big for me in this case already." As I savored another bite of the flavorful pasta. "Can you do me a favor and keep an eye on Michelle? With her coming in late in the game, I have a hunch she may try to pull something."

"Alright, I will. She's pretty reliable, though. We've been working closely, and she hasn't given me any reason to think she'd sabotage anything."

We return to the brother sister relationship we always had. We talked about our days and the house hunt he has been having, and about Tiffany. Steve was getting up from the table after finishing his dinner. "I need to call Tiff and find out about her day. Thanks again for letting me stay with you during the week until we can move in and settle."

"No problem," I said as I got up, the sound of our chairs scraping the floor. "It's great to have you here. It can become a little lonely being by myself. Tell Tiffany I said hello."

He disappeared down the hall, but I caught an "I will" as he left. Moving to the sofa, I settled back with my glass of wine and turned on some music. I selected the adult contemporary station, the mellow tunes providing a soothing backdrop. A love song from my college days played, and I smiled, letting the sentimental melody flood my mind. The stress melted away. Denise would have some excellent thoughts and would help me out. Sighing and smiling again, I thought about tomorrow's coffee date.

Chapter 9

The Smell of Brew exuded a comforting blend of brewed coffee and espresso machines humming. It was a place of activity. The morning chatter was evident as I settled into a corner table with my laptop. Sipping on a latte, I invited Denise to a Zoom call and waited for her to log in. Once again, I needed her expertise and assistance.

"Hey, Denise. How's it going?"

"Great! How about you?"

"I'm doing well, but I do have a favor to ask. You're the only one I trust to handle this right now, along with a friend of mine."

"I'm always happy to help."

I kept talking with Denise, and she agreed to help. After we wrapped up, we said our goodbyes, and I ended the call. A laugh escaped as I closed my laptop.

Jack walked into the café. His presence lifted my mood, and I waved for him to join me.

"Hey! I'm glad you could make it."

He returned my smile, taking a seat across from me. "How's everything going with the case?"

Glancing around, I leaned. "It's progressing. We've uncovered some compelling proof to make a difference, and I have a hunch"

"That's great!" he said. "I've been curious about the details. Maybe we can discuss it over our coffee?"

"I need your help with something crucial."

He nodded, his eyes focused on mine. "Of course, Holli. What can I do?"

"I am requesting samples from the same locations where Joseph took them," I said.

Jack's brow furrowed. "Are you sure about this? It's a sensitive task."

I affirmed, my voice steady. "It's vital to verify if there have been any changes or abnormalities."

He paused, considering my request. "Okay, I'll do it. When do you want the findings?"

"As soon as possible."

"Got it. I'll start right away and keep you updated."

"I can't thank you enough," I said.

He smiled. "I'm here to help."

A comfortable silence stretching out before he spoke.

"Growing up by the coast taught me a lot, you know?" His gaze distant, as if he could still see the waves. "The beauty of it, but also the toll pollution takes. It's what pulled me toward engineering—wanting to do something about it, make even a small difference."

I nodded, understanding the pull of that kind of purpose. "I get that. I've always been drawn to fairness, to helping people through the rough patches life can throw at them. Seeing how deeply legal struggles impacted my family made me realize how much people need advocates."

He looked over at me, a thoughtful smile playing at the corners of his mouth. "So you were driven by that sense of the pursuit of justice, even back then?"

"Yeah, I suppose so," I replied, smiling at the memory. "It's funny. I didn't set out thinking I'd end up here, but it's like all those experiences shaped it for me. Somehow, life pointed me toward a place where I could make a difference."

He chuckled softly. "Funny how life has a way of doing that. Same with me—I didn't start off aiming to be an eco engineer. I just knew I wanted to be part of the solution. Even the small steps, they add up to something."

"Exactly," I said, feeling a warmth in the shared understanding. "It's rewarding, isn't it? Knowing that what you do matters, even in small ways."

Our words faded into a comfortable silence, deepening the connection of shared purpose and parallel paths. We got up to leave and pushed our chairs in and headed for the door.

We walked outside Smell of Brew, sensing it was time to return to our respective responsibilities. We covered a lot, including updates on the case and personal stories.

"I should leave," he said, glancing at his watch. "Let's keep in touch about those sample data."

"Absolutely," I said. "Thanks again for agreeing to help with that. I'll be waiting to hear from you."

I saw him head off down the street. I made my way to my car and headed toward Winston and Associates. The familiar route took me past shops and buildings, bringing me closer to the firm. I walked into my office.

"Good morning, Holli," Amanda said cheerfully. "Have you been productive?"

I gave a faint grin. "It's been quite busy already. Any updates?"

Amanda's expression turned as she bent forward. "There's something you might want to examine. Have you checked the headlines online today?"

I shook my head, curiosity piqued. "No, I haven't. Is there something specific I should be aware of?"

"There's a news report about the Titian's situation. It came out a few minutes ago."

I turned on my computer, and I moved closer to the screen as she navigated to the journalism website. The headline read, "Corporate Fraud Allegations Rock Local Business: Titian Construction Under Investigation."

The anchor reported accusations of environmental violations involving TerraGuard Technologies. Images of the company's headquarters and footage from recent protests of the water contamination flashed across the monitor. I listened to the damning accusations and witnessed the seriousness with which the media outlet covered the story.

"We need to find out who's responsible," I said. "We can't let this damage our negotiations."

Amanda began to walk towards the door. "I'll keep my ear to the ground here. It would be best if you talked to Michelle. She might have insights or spotted something we missed."

I looked at Amanda. "I agree." I hurried down the corridor to Michelle's office without wasting another moment. The importance of our conversation with her still echoed in my mind as I approached her door. I knocked before entering, finding her focused on her computer monitor.

"We have a problem," My voice was urgent.

She looked up, as I informed her of the leaked details and Amanda's concerns. She listened and raced through the potential implications.

"We need to find the source," she said. "Let's start by reviewing all recent communications and access logs. There has to be a trail."

"You can work on the leak's origins. I will do damage control with McAllister, Justin and Davis".

"Agreed! I will be right on this, and if I have any details, I will let you know."

"Let's reconvene," I said, the click of my heels echoing down the hallway as I left Michelle's office. My mind raced to call Justin.

I gathered my thoughts, but my mind was still occupied with the urgency of the Sports Alliance and Youth Education circumstance. I grasped that the following steps were crucial. Ensuring the retesting of the samples was expedited and accurate would be paramount in addressing the allegations.

I glanced at the clock on my desk. It was nearing midday and I realized I needed to touch base with Michelle, Steve and Amanda. I exited and went down the hall, and approached Michelle's office door and saw Steve and Amanda inside, intensely talking about the situation. He looked up as I entered, his expression focused.

"Holli," He motioned for me to join them. "We were discussing the latest developments. She found something you should see."

Curious and apprehensive, I proceeded to her desk. She opened her laptop. She turned the screen toward me. She pointed to the news on the monitor.

"Take a look at this," she said.

I read through the headline and the first few paragraphs, feeling a sinking sensation in my stomach. The article detailed allegations linking the Youth Sports and Education Alliance to environmental violations and implicating damaging practices.

"This is not good," I said, thinking of Justin and the impact this may have on his charity.

Michelle said, "Justin's going to need reassurance, we must be proactive in our response."

I tried to gather my thoughts amidst the escalating circumstance. "I spoke to him. He worries about how this will affect the charity's reputation."

Steve leaned forward. "We have to confirm the retest results. That should be our first step."

"I'll coordinate with Amanda to ensure the testing is expedited."

"We need to begin drafting a statement for Justin. He needs to grasp we're taking this."

I bit my bottom lip. "Let's also loop in our PR consultant. We'll require a unified approach to handling the media."

She grinned. "I'll start writing the announcement with her on the details."

"Let's move fast," I said, meeting each other's eyes. "We can't afford any missteps."

During the strategy discussion, my phone rang, breaking the intense focus in the room. I glanced at the caller ID—it was Jack. With a quick apologetic look. I answered the call.

"Hey, what's the update?" I kept my voice steady despite the importance.

"Holli, I've got the results. They came back negative. There's no contamination detected."

A wave of relief washed over me, visible enough that Michelle raised an eyebrow in question. I gave a subtle thumb-up, signaling that it was positive news. "That's great. Thank you for your swift action on this."

"I understand how critical it was," he said. I've already prepared the report. I'll send it to Amanda right away."

"Perfect," I said, I looked directly at Amanda. "Amanda will look out for it. Thanks again, Jack. This helps us a lot."

I turned back, unable to contain my smile. "The samples are clean. Jack 's sending the detailed draft to her now."

Michelle sighed while Amanda checked her email. "That's a huge relief. Now we can focus on drafting the statement for Justin."

Steve looked at us. "Let's keep moving forward with the plan. This buys us some breathing room."

I made my way to my office, with a sense of immediacy propelling. The corridor was bustling with colleagues deep in conversation or rushing to their next meetings. I passed, exchanged quick nods and brief smiles, but stayed focused on the task ahead.

I paused at my door to collect my thoughts before entering. The room was neat and organized, contrasting with the chaotic situation outside. The documents scattered across my desk, reminders of ongoing cases and tasks that demanded attention.

I settled into my chair, the familiar creak comforting in its routine. Placing my phone on silent mode, I opened my laptop to review the latest updates and emails. The urgency of the morning's events lingered. Jack's reassuring news echoing in my mind, a sense of relief and purpose filled the air.

I began to draft a detailed email to Justin outlining the results of the sample tests and our planned steps moving forward. Each word was chosen, aiming to convey both clarity and reassurance. The office hum faded into the background as I typed, replaced by the quiet determination to end this crisis.

I leaned back in my chair. "What a day!" I said to myself. "It is not over."

I focused on strategizing our approach with the city lawsuit and prepare for TerraGuard's suit as well. I was confident in our preparation and strategy.

I considered Justin's charity, and I wondered how the impending publicity might affect it. With a solid plan and the expertise of our PR team, I remained optimistic about navigating the challenge.

I picked up my phone, and then I composed a text to Jack.

"Thanks for your help today. We're close to wrapping this up, but I need some info to confirm my hunch. Interested in grabbing dinner soon?"

A few minutes later, his reply came. It was straightforward yet warm.

"You're welcome. Yes, soon."

A smile spread across my face. Building a friendship with him felt natural, and I appreciated the comfort and camaraderie he brought. Perhaps there was potential for more between us, but for now, I enjoyed the simplicity of our growing connection.

My phone buzzed with a notification. Denise was calling. I accepted the video call, and her face filled my screen.

"Holli, I've got the data you asked for. It's more damning than we thought."

My heart raced a little. "Go on?" I leaned forward.

"The financial records show a clear pattern of transactions that link the shell companies to him. The offshore accounts, the shifting of funds—it's all there. This isn't a minor oversight; it's deliberate."

I absorbed her words. "That's exactly what we needed. This is critical for us."

"There's more. I found correspondence that suggests he was aware of the implications and went ahead anyway. The emails are explicit. He orchestrated a plan to cover his tracks, but not well enough. There's proof of a bankruptcy filing to hide the financial discrepancies. It's all part of the same scheme."

"Can you send me copies of all this?" I said. "We must show this evidence, but it will be a game-changer."

Denise smiled. "I'm sending everything to you now. Be cautious. It can jeopardize your strategy."

"I understand. We'll handle it with the utmost care. Thank you for your hard work on this."

I took a moment to digest the weight of the uncovered proof. My gut was correct, and the little clues I picked up pointed towards the same conclusion. The implications were staggering, and the meticulous planning to present it would be crucial. I needed to bring law enforcement, John Knox, into the loop.

I looked at my phone and dialed John's number, the familiar tones ringing in my ear. He answered after the second ring.

"Hey there!! What's up?" His voice was calm but alert.

This would be a difficult conversation. " How are you doing? We haven't talked for a while."

"I'm good. Keeping myself busy. There are lots of bad guys to catch."

"Speaking of not-so-good guys, I need to review some important details with you. This is significant. Can you meet with me at the station as soon as possible?" I asked.

There was a brief pause before John said, "Can you be here in twenty minutes?"

"Yes, I can."

"I will see you then."

I hung up. The following steps would be crucial, and having John's insight would be invaluable.

I drove to meet him. My mind raced. The streets blurred into a monotony of traffic lights and intersections. This wasn't about financial misconduct; it was deliberate deception.

Pulling into the parking lot, I thought about how we would present the proof. It had to be done, ensuring the element of surprise. I grabbed the folder containing copies of the documents and headed into the building, my steps quick and purposeful.

He looked up as I entered. I wasted no time, laying the file on the table between us.

John picked up the file and gave a half smile.

I continued, "These records outline a clear pattern of transactions and emails implicating him. It's all here," I said, flipping through the pages to highlight key points.

He examined the files, his brow furrowing as he read. After a few moments, he looked up at me. "Are you sure this is accurate?"

"Yes, it came from Denise through Samantha."

"This changes everything," I witnessed the gears turning in his mind, formulating a new strategy.

"If we play this right, we can turn this entire matter around."

His expression resolute. "We'll need to prepare for a potential backlash. If this goes public too soon, it may jeopardize our efforts."

"I agree. We have the advantage of surprise."

We spent the next hour reviewing the details and discussing how to incorporate the data into a presentation. He was meticulous, considering every possible angle.

I will present the proof at a meeting with McAllister and Davis at 3 p.m. I got up and move towards the door.

"I will be there. We still make a good team," he said

I approached the door, "Yes, we do. Thank you for the help. I owe you one."

Back at Winston and Associates, I headed straight to Amanda's cubicle, determined to update her on the new developments. She was on the phone as I approached, her voice calm yet focused. Catching sight of me, she wrapped up the call with a quick, "Thanks, I'll follow up on that shortly." Setting the phone down, she turned to me, her full attention ready.

"We've got him," I said, handing her the folder. She skimmed through the documents, her eyes widening as she took in the contents.

"This is huge," she said, looking up at me. "How did you get all this?"

"Denise, through Samantha," I said. "Sam dug deeper and forward it to Denise."

"I'll get the PR team on standby. We must control the narrative once this goes public," Amanda said as she headed out the door.

I looked at Steve and Michelle. "I just got back from seeing John, and together we formulated a plan. all we have to do is set up a meeting. Looking at Amanda I asked, "Can you set up a meeting for McAllister and be sure to invite Davis. We will need to be sure to disclose these findings."

Michelle looked at me, "do you think he will deny it?"

I responded, "He better not, the proof is right here."

We spent the next few hours coordinating our efforts and confirming everything was in place. It was late when I left the office, but I felt satisfied.

This situation had taken unexpected turns, and was far from over, but we were ahead of the game for the first time.

Chapter 10

The morning light seeped through the blinds, glowing across my cluttered desk and open laptop. I cradled a steaming cup of coffee, my mind racing through the implications of the damning evidence Denise had uncovered.

A knock on the door interrupted my intense focus.

"Holli, we need to talk. There's a new development regarding the case."

Setting the papers aside, my brow wrinkled as I met Michelle's eyes. "What's happened?"

She closed the door behind her. "Justin called. He's frantic about the coverage linking the charity to the environmental violations. He wants to meet with you right away."

The timing couldn't have been worse, but Justin's concerns were valid and needed to be addressed to safeguard our legal strategy and reputation.

"I will call him in an hour." My voice steady despite the mounting challenges. "In the meantime, gather the team. We need to prepare for any fallout from the media."

Her eyes reflected empathy and readiness for action. "I'll bring everyone together."

I got up from my desk, an impulse convincing me to stop her. "Wait."

Her look was now tinged with curiosity and concern as she made her way to the sofa in my office. I picked up the folder containing the discovered findings and handed it to her.

"Take a look at this," I said, watching her flip through the pages, her brows furrowing with each revelation. "Denise uncovered these records and emails. It's damning proof linking him to misconduct."

Michelle's eyes widened as she absorbed the implications. "Is this... is this true?"

"Yes, It's all there. We will present this today at 3 pm. If you want to be part of the team handling this, now's the time to dive in."

She nodded slowly, her focus shifting from the papers to me. "I'm in. What about Steve?"

Letting out a sigh, I sat next to her. "I will tell him later this morning. He was up late talking with his wife, and I didn't want to disturb him as I was leaving."

She got up to leave and was almost out the door, when she looked at me, "Thank you for trusting me with this."

I smiled, "No problem."

Sitting at my desk, I sighed and dialed Justin's number. My mind raced with the situation's urgency, but maintaining a calm demeanor was crucial to reassure him.

"Holli," Justin said, his voice tight with tension.

"I wanted to update you. We're working on a PR strategy to address the recent media coverage. I've contacted all parties involved and we're waiting to hear back. It looks like we'll have something more concrete within 24 hours."

There was a brief pause on the other end of the line before he responded, his tone betraying a mix of relief and gratitude. "Thank you. This means a lot to me and the team. We've been worried about how this may impact everything we've built."

"I understand. We're on it. I'll keep you updated every step of the way."

"I appreciate your swift action on this."

I sensed an easing of the tension that had gripped him since the news broke.

"Thank you, Holli," he said. "I await your update. Take care."

"You, too. Don't worry about the fields. We can start scheduling them again. We'll get through this."

A small, grateful chuckle came from him. "That's a relief. Thanks again."

"Absolutely," I affirmed, a smile spreading across my face despite the challenges ahead. "Talk to you soon."

We said our goodbyes, ending the call with cautious optimism. I took a moment to gather my thoughts. The day had been a whirlwind of urgent calls, strategic planning, and crucial updates. With Justin's reassurance and plans in motion for the PR fix, I returned to the immediate tasks. I bit my bottom lip, uneasy with the fact that I often had to withhold information from people. Keeping things to myself felt like an occupational hazard I couldn't escape.

Steve walked into my office. His presence was a welcome interruption, a reminder of the team's cohesion amidst the day's intensity.

"Holli," he said, curious yet composed. "Michelle sent me here. What's going on?"

I motioned for him to join me at the table, where I had laid out the files Denise had provided earlier. I began outlining the findings—the transactions, emails, and other proof.

He listened as he absorbed the gravity of the situation. His background in investigative work made him adept at dissecting complex information and I valued his analytical approach.

"This is substantial. She did a thorough job."

"The 3 p.m. meeting in the conference room will conclude our discussion. Will you be able to attend?"

I sat at my desk, the upcoming discussion with Davis and McAllister bearing down on me. The papers lay scattered, revealing the intricate web of deceit that was woven. I reviewed them one last time, bracing myself for the confrontation.

Sighing, I rose from my chair and walked over to the window. I stared out at the cityscape below. Justin's charity resonated in my mind. It was essential to the community; they would be able to play on those fields soon. His and the charity's reputation would come through this with minimal damage. All I thought about was what loomed ahead and that someone was going to jail today because of it.

The partnership opportunity flickered in my mind—a testament not to ambition but to the importance of this case in defining my career. I wondered if I valued my job as a partner attorney or the justice unveiled.

I closed my eyes, taking a moment to gather my thoughts. I turned away from the window.

Steve and Michelle entered my office with solemn expressions.

"Are you ready for this?" Steve's concern for younger sister was evident.

Michelle settled on the couch. "If anyone can pull this off, it's you."

I leaned back in my chair. "John will be waiting outside for his dramatic entrance."

"Any developments?" he asked.

I looked at my cell phone, noticing the time, I rose from my desk to guide them towards the door. "No, nothing new.

Let's head to the conference room. Davis and McAllister should be showing up."

We arrived in conference room #1, and I flicked on the lights. We began setting up and arranging documents and laptops.

"We need to ensure every detail is covered," I double-checked the agenda on my tablet. Steve and Michelle nodded in agreement.

"You've got this," Michelle said, placing a stack of files on the table.

John joined us moments later, bringing a calm resolve to the room as we reviewed our strategy.

John then left the room and took his place outside in the hallway.

Davis was the first to enter, his demeanor purposeful.

He glanced at me, his look lingering before he spoke. "Holli, are you ready to settle this?"

I met his gaze. "I believe we have a strong case. Settling is the best option to avoid complications."

Davis leaned forward; his expression thoughtful. "I understand your perspective. We need to consider all angles." He sifted through the stack of documents on the table, his gaze with intent. "This case is complex, but the goal remains the same—settle if we can. Avoid the spotlight and the risks that come with it."

I studied the evidence spread before us, my mind ticking through the potential impacts. "A settlement keeps things quieter, but we need leverage. If the opposing side thinks they hold all the power, they won't budge."

A noise echoed from the conference room door. The door swung and McAllister strode into the room.

Davis and I sat at the head of the long conference room table, documents spread neatly before us, a quiet air of readiness between us. As McAllister entered, his gaze swept the room, each step calculated to convey authority.

"Good afternoon, everyone," he announced, his voice calm but intentional. He glanced our way, a subtle acknowledgment that didn't linger.

"Hi," I said, gesturing to an open chair. "Please, have a seat."

McAllister settled in, leaning back in the chair with a controlled ease that hinted at defensiveness beneath his calm exterior. His expression remained neutral, his eyes steady, revealing nothing.

I began the conversation as I walked to the other side of the conference table. "Our best option is to settle—and fast." I said, leaning forward, hands pressed against the table. "Drawing this out benefits no one. The other side wants a public apology on record." My jaw tightened slightly.

"They want the optics, the image of a 'win,'" Davis replied, looking at the stack of notes we'd gathered. "We may be able to shape that to your advantage. The apology keeps things clean if we handle it right. But we can't have them thinking we'll bend on everything."

I added "A public statement closes the door without dragging you through the mud. Settle, issue the apology, and close this out with as little fire as possible."

McAllister's brow furrowed as he processed my statement. "An apology implies guilt." Each of his words were firm and deliberate. "We followed every guideline and regulation. There must be a way to resolve this without escalating."

The tension in the room thickened. McAllister's stance was clear: any public apology would open the door to vulnerability, to implied fault, and that wasn't something he was willing to accept.

I leaned forward, catching McAllister's eye with purpose. "The apology isn't about guilt—it's about optics. We've seen how public perception can turn fast, and we need to get ahead of that. The quicker we take responsibility, the quicker we move past this."

McAllister's jaw tightened, his focus shifting from Davis back to me. I didn't back down. "This isn't about bending the truth or admitting fault," I continued. "This is about acknowledging the impact, even if it's unintentional. It'll put us in a position of strength, not weakness."

Davis nodded subtly, giving his silent support, which added weight to my words. McAllister's shoulders relaxed just a fraction, considering.

"We craft the apology on our terms," I added. "We control the narrative, keep it concise, professional. No admissions, just a show of responsibility. That diffuses the public pressure, makes this a non-story."

McAllister finally exhaled, his rigid stance softening. "Fine," he said after a long pause, conceding. "But let's make it clear, we're not guilty.

Let's finalize all the details and move forward with the rest of our day."
He started to push back his chair, already halfway standing. "I'll leave
you to it. Heading back to my office. Well done, Holli—I look forward
to reviewing the report."

"Hold on, Mr. McAllister," I said, reaching out slightly to catch his
attention. "We still have a few more issues to go over with you. It's
important we cover everything before moving forward."

He hesitated, a trace of impatience crossing his face before he settled
back into his chair, folding his hands and waiting expectantly.

"We can discuss the apology later, but we still have lingering issues-
allegations of fiscal problems and bankruptcy."

McAllister's jaw tightened as he gripped the edge of the conference
table, eyes narrowing as if to steady himself against the words. He
glanced between us, a flicker of disbelief crossing his face.

"What do you mean, fiscal problems and bankruptcy? I gave the
current financials to you last week. We are very strong financially."
His voice dropped, each word clipped.

I slid a folder with latest report across the table, pointing to the
highlighted sections. "There are concerns circulating allegations that
we're skirting the edge of financial ruins.

His hand trembled slightly as he grabbed the report, scanning it
quickly. A muscle twitched in his jaw. He looked up, eyes sharp,
darting from Davis to me.

"Unbelievable."

"We investigated your company," I said. "We uncovered some
questionable practices that were confirmed last night."

Michelle rose from her chair, her gaze fixed on the two men.
"We've gathered detailed bank statements, income reports, and audits
indicating economic troubles at Titan. There's evidence of substantial
fund transfers to the Cayman Islands."

His brow creased. "The Cayman Islands? I've never authorized any accounts there. How is this possible?"

She interjected, "We've also traced internal emails revealing the movement and intended use of these funds."

"We have corroborating testimony from a whistleblower who provided crucial details and documentation as evidence," I continued.

Michelle added, "Titan has officially filed for Chapter 11 bankruptcy protection."

Steve stood and joined us. "Regarding Chapter 11, it took effort, but we've obtained court records confirming Titan's filing."

McAllister's confusion deepened. "So Titan is bankrupt?"

"Unfortunately, yes."

My attention shifted to Davis as I handed the files to McAllister. "You wanted me to investigate because you believed McAllister would be implicated in fraud."

Davis's once smug look turned into visible concern.

"I almost fell for it. Something you said in your office yesterday sparked a hunch in me. You and McAllister 'went way back.' That's when I looked beyond the surface. If I hadn't, there were plans in motion to have Mr. McAllister guilty of fraud, and going to jail. You needed the case settled to avoid further investigation And discover your plan. You even went as far as to plant arsenic near sights you thought I would be collecting samples. However you did not read the report from TerraGuard on where the original site for the testing were. We retested and they are clear."

I paused, taking a drink of water before continuing. "When I began the case, I assumed, you both knew each other professionally. So when I discovered you went 'way back', I did some digging into your cases and clients over the years. My sources found a signed delegation of financial authority with external consultants that had no expiration date."

"What is that?" McAllister asked.

Michelle walked over. "It's like a Power of Attorney for companies, allowing someone to handle finances, and make financial transaction on behalf of the company."

"I find that hard to believe," said McAllister. "I've never authorized such a thing. How could this happen without my knowledge?"

Michelle stepped in, holding up papers. "We have the signed forms right here. They began when Mr. Davis was your lawyer a decade ago."

I turned to McAllister and Davis. "Does the name Paige Stevens mean anything to you?"

McAllister straightened in his chair. "She's my personal assistant."

Michelle leaned forward, her tone sharp. "Well, it seems Mr. Davis knows her quite well—very well, in fact. They've been communicating for over a decade. The most recent email, sent just last week, reads, 'I'm almost done moving the funds, and he'll be in a prison cell soon.' A word of advice, Mr. Davis, next time, encrypt your emails."

She glanced at McAllister. "Ms. Stevens has been using your work email to send these messages. Not only that, but she's been falsifying financial records and sending them to you, carefully maintaining the illusion that Titan was financially stable."

"You orchestrated this scheme, moving funds over time. The plan was to implicate him and disappear. Multiple shell companies were used to obscure the trail."

"I had no idea," McAllister said, shaking his head. "This is outrageous."

Reviewing the additional files, Steve said, "We've traced the money flow and have proof linking it to various accounts. It's quite intricate, and it is over $60 million"

"You can't prove any of this," Davis said.

Just then, the conference room door opened, and John stepped in, pausing by the entrance. His presence filled the space, a silent acknowledgment he was there.

I moved to the other side of the table. "Yes, we can, and we have. We have it all documented, both on paper and electronically. We've contacted the Financial Crimes Enforcement Network and they'll be here tomorrow."

"I misjudged you, Holli. I thought you might do anything to make a partner. You had settled the matter when I told you the prestige, money, and caseload would be yours."

I stepped closer, making sure he would catch sight of my face. "You underestimated me. The truth matters more to me than any of those things. It took me a while to realize that."

"You do not know who you are dealing with," Davis said

Davis's warning hung in the air, his eyes cold and steady.

A hint of defiance stirred within me, and I held his gaze. "Maybe not," I replied, voice calm but firm. "But I know exactly who I am—and what I stand for."

He tried reaching for the door, but John intercepted and put him in handcuffs. He let out a sigh as John read him his Miranda Rights as they exited the room.

McAllister glanced around the room, his expression contemplative as he took a moment to absorb the atmosphere. "This is a mess. I need to consult with my legal team," he muttered to himself, shaking his head slightly.

After meeting the eyes of everyone present, he stood and left the room, his company's dire straits evident in his demeanor.

Watching him leave, I let the moment settle. Taking a deep breath, I sat down. The reality of what had transpired hit me like a wave. I had uncovered massive fraud, confronted a powerful man, and held my ground. The enormity of it all was almost overwhelming.

Michelle sat beside me. "Are you okay?"

I put my hand on hers. "Yes, I'm fine."

Amanda rushed into the room, her eyes curious. "I saw Davis leave the building. Was he in cuffs?"

"He sure was!" I said.

Sitting at my desk, I watched Amanda and Michelle walk in and settle on the couch. I greeted them with a grateful nod. "Thank you both for being here."

"I'm still trying to process everything," Michelle said, her voice tinged with excitement.

She turned to me with a thoughtful look. "It's hard to believe he was involved for so long and waited."

My phone rang, and I answered the phone. "Hello?"

"Hello Holli... Its John."

"Hey, how's it going?"

"It's going well. I wanted to inform you that Davis's in the holding cell and might make bail. Keep your doors locked until FCEN takes him tomorrow."

"Thanks for letting me know."

"You're welcome. Take care."

"I will, and you too." I ended the call and relayed the information to Amanda and Michelle.

Amanda looked at me with concern. "Do you want to stay over at my place tonight?"

I shook my head. "No, I think I'll be okay."

"Alright," Amanda said

"Go home for the day. I think we've earned it."

Amanda was leaving the room. "You don't have to tell me twice. Meet up with you tomorrow!"

Michelle gathered her things with a smile. "See you later."

They left, and I settled back at my desk, my phone began to ring again. It was Jack.

"Hey, I was thinking about calling you."

"Really? How did it go today," he said.

"Emotional. I think I'm going to head home."

"I think that's a good idea. How about dinner tomorrow? There's a great place on Main Street."

A slight grin crept onto my face. "Perfect. I am looking forward to it."

"Okay, bye."

"Goodbye."

After ending the call with him, I packed up my belongings, organized my desk, and ensured everything was set for the next day. I walked outside. I was relieved the day was finally over.

The cool breeze was refreshing as I took a deep breath, releasing the tension that had built up throughout the day. I looked forward to the evening, I cherished the sense of accomplishment from today's small victory.

Thoughts of dinner plans with Jack provided a welcome distraction—a chance to unwind after the intensity. I arrived at my house, I recognized that today marked a significant turning point.

Steve had gone home to be with his family added to the peaceful atmosphere. I realized tomorrow would bring more tasks and challenges, but I was satisfied with a well-done job.

Chapter 11

I sat in my quiet house, the faint hum of the city seeping through the windows. I couldn't shake the words Davis had thrown at me in the conference room. "I thought you'd do anything to make a partner." The accusation echoed in my mind, gnawing at me. Was he right? Had my ambition blinded me to the true nature of the case? Had I been chosen because I was seen as manipulated, driven by a hunger for success?

I walked to the kitchen, poured a glass of water, and stared out the window, the city lights twinkling like distant stars. The day's adrenaline had worn off, leaving a void in my chest. I had desired to be a partner, prove myself, and climb to the top—at what cost? I had given up a lot. I had sacrificed much of my time for other pursuits. I've always loved singing, painting, and starting a family.

Sinking into the sofa, I closed my eyes and let my ideas drift back to why I had become a lawyer in the first place. It wasn't for prestige or money. I chose this path because I wanted to help people. I remembered the situations that inspired me during law school. There were instances where lawyers fought for the underdog, those who couldn't fight for themselves.

My mind wandered to Justin. I viewed the ease on his face when I reassured him that we were working on a strategy to protect the charity's reputation. I had chosen this career to understand how my work impacted someone's life. It's not about the title of partner but the difference I can make.

Davis's words, meant to wound, had instead reminded me of my true purpose. I wasn't manipulated but driven by a more bottomless, profound ambition—to seek justice and help those in need.

The path ahead wouldn't be easy, but I was more confident about why I was on it. I would continue to fight for the people who needed me, and in doing so, I realized I would find the meaning of success.

I got ready and made my way into the office. It was just like any other day. I greeted the security guard and headed to the elevator. I couldn't help but think about Davis's words.

Walking into my office, I was struck by how normal everything seemed. The cluttered desk had the same view from the window, starkly contrasting my turmoil. I set my bag down and turned on my laptop, the screen flickering to life with emails and notifications.

Moments later, Amanda walked with a bright smile on her face. "Morning, Holli." She was holding a stack of papers.

"Anything urgent?"

"Yes," she said, her grin fading as she glanced at the files. "You have messages from McAllister. He wants to schedule the apology as soon as possible. There are also calls from the city and the counsel from TerraGuard."

I sighed, running a hand through my hair. "Alright, let's start with McAllister. Can you reach him on the line for me?"

"Of course," she said, heading to the telephone on my desk. She dialed, and I took a moment to organize my thoughts. We must address this.

She handed me the phone. "Mr. McAllister, it's Holli."

"Thank you for getting back to me," McAllister's voice came through. "I wanted to discuss the statement. We need to do this right."

I said, my mind racing with ideas. "Let's go over the details and make sure we're prepared for any questions that might come up."

As we talked, I glanced at Amanda, who was sorting through more messages and paperwork. The city and the attorney from TerraGuard hold off for now. One step at a time, I reminded myself.

After finalizing the plan with McAllister, I hung up and turned to her. "Alright, what's next?"

"The city wants to discuss the media coverage and how it's affecting their partnership with the charity. The counsel from TerraGuard has some updates on their end."

"Got it," I continued. I'll call the city first. Can you set up a call later today?"

"Will do." She left my office for her desk.

I picked up the phone to call, and dialed. I prepared myself for the conversation. The recent coverage caused some concern, and I wanted to reassure them that we were handling the situation.

"Good morning, this is Holli Buchannan,"

"Good morning, Holli. This is Sharon from the Department of Water and Power. I understand you have some new test results at the community football fields?"

I got up, and looked out the window. "Yes, I do. I can transmit them over to you. Would this take care of the lawsuit, violation and fines?"

"If everything is in order and we can verify the result, there will be no problem," Sharon said.

I moved back to my desk. "I will forward them over right away. I have your email address, and you should receive them within the next 10 minutes."

"It's not a problem," she said. "I will have them looked at, and we need to inform McAllister and any other plaintiffs."

"Perfect," I said. "Thank you so much."

I verified and said goodbye, typed the message, attached the document, and pressed send.

Amanda arrived at my office door, agitated. "I tried to set up an appointment with the lawyer from TerraGuard today. They insisted on speaking with you. They said it's urgent."

I frowned, glancing at the clock. "Alright, put them through. Let's scrutinize what they have to say."

She connected the call, and moments later, I was speaking with the lead counsel from TerraGuard.

"Holli, this is Mark Davis. We need to discuss the deformation suit with Titian Construction." Mark's voice was brisk and businesslike.

I looked at her. "Hi. We had some developments yesterday and McAllister has agreed to statement if TerraGuard will drop this matter."

"That's a smart move. It will help diffuse the situation. Here's what will happen. He apologizes, and the open acknowledgment should be sufficient to restore credibility in our company."

I experienced a wave of solace. "That sounds like a solid plan. I'll make him understand the importance of his statement and that it needs to be sincere and comprehensive."

"Good. The sooner, the better."

"I'll coordinate with him and the PR team to schedule the announcement," I said. "We'll make sure all major media outlets cover it."

"Perfect," he said.

I looked at Amanda and gave a thumbs up. "Thanks"

I hung up the phone and leaned back in my chair. "I think we are close to having this completed. I will need to call Justin and inform him," I smiled.

She grinned back. "I will talk with McAllister and let you speak with Justin."

I sat up and returned Amanda's smile. "This will be easy."

"I will leave you to it," she said as she left my office.

I settled in, ready to tackle the tasks ahead. I sifted through emails and reviewed notes, and an email from Denise caught my eye. Curious, I opened it.

Holli,

I just learned about Davis's arrest and wanted to congratulate you on your success. You followed through on the integrity issue and didn't let ambition blind you to the truth. I'm impressed by your dedication to justice and your ability to navigate such a complex situation.

Your determination to uncover the truth and your refusal to be manipulated have not gone unnoticed. I understand how challenging it can be to stay true to oneself in this field, and you have shown remarkable strength.

With that in mind, I wanted to extend an opportunity to you. My organization seeks someone with your skills, drive, and ethical standards. We believe you would be a valuable addition to our firm. We can discuss this further at your earliest convenience.

I am looking forward to hearing from you.

Best,

Denise.

I leaned back in my chair while absorbing the words. Denise's compliment and recognition meant a lot from a person I respect. Her acknowledgment of my integrity and dedication was like a validation of the path I had chosen.

The job opportunity was unexpected. I had always seen myself advancing within my current company, working towards becoming a partner. Her proposition made me pause and reconsider my future. Joining her can be a fresh start, a new challenge, and a chance to align me with a team that values ethical practices.

I wanted time to think this over, so I typed a quick response.

Denise,

Thank you so much for your kind words and congratulations. It means a lot coming from you. I appreciate your recognition of my efforts and integrity.

Your job opportunity is both flattering and intriguing. I would love to discuss this further and explore potential opportunities. I'll reach out soon to set up a time for us to talk.

Thanks again for your support and encouragement.

Best,

Holli

I decided to keep this to myself for now. I didn't want to create distractions while wrapping up and finalizing matters with Justin's charity, but the idea intrigued me.

The firm was a sports agency, and my work involved representing athletes in contract negotiations. I found this field both familiar and rewarding.

Taking the job would mean relocating to a new city six hours away. I wanted time to review the offer letter and reply to her soon.

I picked up my phone and called Justin. I was excited because this would be a positive conversation.

"It's Holli," I began, trying to keep my tone light despite the urgency.

"Thanks," he said, his voice filled with comfort. "I've been fielding calls all morning about this mess. What's the latest?"

"I have good information," I said, eager to share it. "The city agreed to nullify the violation. They will issue a statement later today confirming that the fields are cleared for use again."

A brief pause was on the other end of the line. "That's huge. I can't thank you enough for your efforts on this."

"I'm glad I can help. You've worked so hard to build this charity. Things are turning around."

He chuckled. "It's been a rollercoaster, that's for sure. I owe you one."

"Just doing my job," I said with a smile.

"I'll spread the word and tell them they're back in action."

I leaned up from my desk. "Talk soon."

Moments like these reminded me why I became an attorney: to make a positive impact on people like Justin.

Michelle and I enjoyed a rare lunch break at a cozy cafe. The sun cast a pleasant warmth over the outdoor patio where we sat. We chatted about the latest office gossip, savoring our sandwiches and the brief respite from work.

"So, any plans for the weekend?" she asked, sipping her iced tea.

I smiled. "Not much, just planning to relax and catch up on reading. How about you?"

"Thinking about a hike if the weather stays nice. It's been a while since I've had a trek in the woods

We continued our light-hearted conversation. My phone buzzed on the table. I looked at the screen and spotted Jack 's name. Excusing myself, I answered the call.

"Hey."

"Hey, Holli," Jack said, his voice warm. "I was wondering what time I should pick you up?"

I glanced at Michelle, who pretended not to eavesdrop with a mischievous grin. "I'll meet you there. It's easier that way, and I have a few things to wrap up at the office."

"Looking forward to it," he said.

"Me too. See you soon," I said before hanging up.

She raised an eyebrow as I put my phone down. "Dinner plans?"

I laughed. "Yeah, Jack and I are meeting up tonight."

"He's a good guy," she said. "You two have connected."

"It'll be a wonderful way to end a crazy week."

We continued our lunch when the café's television caught our attention. Mounted in the corner, it was tuned to the local channel. The headline scrolling across the bottom of the screen read, "Breaking news from Titian Construction."

"Looks like we might be able to catch it live," Michelle said, nodding toward the TV.

We both focused on the screen as the anchor introduced the segment. "We now go to the press conference where McAllister, CEO of Titan, is set to issue a statement."

The camera cut to him standing behind a podium, looking tense but composed. He took a heavy breath before speaking.

"Ladies and gentlemen, I stand to apologize for our company's statements about the water contamination at the football fields. Our leadership should never deflect responsibility and implicate TerraGuard. They were never involved in any of the testing. I want to take full blame for the mistakes I made. Our company did not uphold the standards we set for ourselves, and for that I am sorry."

We exchanged a glance, our food forgotten. McAllister's sincerity was evident.

He stepped away from the podium, and the camera panned back to the anchor, who provided some additional commentary on the apology.

"Well, there it is," Michelle said, breaking the silence. "He did it."

"Yeah. It's a step in the right direction."

We resumed our lunch. Knowing that McAllister had taken responsibility was a significant milestone, and it was good to witness it firsthand.

McAllister's statement validated us and gave us a glimpse of our work potential's positive impact, but the day was far from over.

I stepped into my office, and Amanda approached me.

"Holli, the partners have called a meeting in the conference room. They want to meet with you," she said.

My heart skipped a beat. My mind racing with possibilities. I tried to steady my nerves.

Inside, three senior partners—Mr. Reynolds, Ms. Ellis, and Mr. Thompson—were seated around the large table, their expressions encouraging. I closed the door behind me and sat.

"Holli," Mr. Reynolds started, "we've been following your recent work on handling the Davis matter."

Ms. Ellis continued, "Your tenacity, legal acumen, and unwavering integrity have not gone unnoticed. You demonstrated remarkable skill and dedication under immense pressure."

Mr. Thompson eyes locked on mine. "In light of your exemplary performance and the values you uphold, we invite you to become a Junior Partner at Winston and Associates."

I was speechless. The words hung in the air, almost surreal. I had worked for this moment, but hearing it articulated by the senior partners made it all the more real.

"I don't know what to say. Thank you. This means so much to me."

Mr. Reynolds smiled. "You've earned it, Holli. Your commitment to justice and exceptional legal skills have proven you are more than capable of this responsibility."

Ms. Ellis added, "We do not doubt you will continue to be an asset and inspire others with your dedication."

I sat back in my chair. "How would my caseload be affected?"

Ms. Ellis answered, "As a Junior Partner, you would take on more high-profile cases that required expertise. You will engage in strategic thinking. You will also understand our client's needs. You would lead from start to finish, ensuring every aspect is handled. The pressure to deliver successful outcomes would be higher, but so would the rewards.

"Besides managing significant matters, you would be crucial in mentoring junior associates. I understand you learned from your mentors. It is your turn to guide and support the next generation of lawyers at Winston and Associates," Reynolds added.

"Can I have some time to think about it?"

Ms. Ellis smiled at me. "Yes, take some time, but not too long."

I grinned at her as I prepared to stand up to leave. "Thank you all for this incredible opportunity," I said, addressing the three senior partners before me. "I'm honored by your confidence in my abilities."

I gathered my things and stood. Mr. Thompson said, "Holli, whatever you decide, we respect your decision. You've earned this."

"Thank you. That means a lot to me," I said, giving them all an appreciative smile exiting the conference room.

Walking down the hallway, my mind buzzed with thoughts about the meeting. I wanted to find some clarity to weigh my options.

I settled back into my office chair, the morning gathering with the senior partners still fresh. Amanda bustled in with a stack of documents, her usual cheerful demeanor contrasting the atmosphere lingering in my workspace.

One subject line stood out among the emails awaiting my attention: "Congratulations and Updates." Curious, I clicked to open it. The familiar name of Hannah Patterson, a former colleague from my early years, greeted me.

Dear Holli,

I hope this message finds you well amidst the whirlwind of your recent achievements. I've admired your career and congratulate you on your outstanding performance handling the Davis case. Your dedication and unwavering integrity have always been your defining qualities.

On a personal note, I wanted to share some news—I've taken on a new role as managing partner at a firm specializing in sports law. Your journey inspired me to stay true to my principles in this demanding field.

I'd love to catch up sometime soon. Perhaps we can talk next week? I want to learn more about your experiences.

I wish you continued success and look forward to reconnecting.

Warm regards,

Hannah.

I reread Hannah's email. Her words resonated, reminding me of the mentor bonds forged in the early stages of my work. It also ignited a flicker of curiosity about alternative career paths.

Leaning back in my chair, I reflected on her journey and my aspirations. It reminded me that I can impact wherever I am, and it's fulfilling to think about it.

I replied, expressing my gratitude for her kind words and enthusiasm for catching up. I couldn't shake the dilemma of Denise's proposal looming in the background. Denise had been more than just a mentor—she had been a guiding force throughout my work, someone I respected.

The prospect of leaving my current firm to join her team was exciting and daunting. I considered the potential of the new attorneys I would guide and nurture.

My notions were interrupted by the gentle chime of my phone alarm, reminding me of my dinner plans with Jack. Gathering my things, I prepared to leave, my mind still buzzing with the decisions ahead.

I reached for the doorknob, and Amanda burst into the office, excitement radiating from her. "Holli, I just learned the news about the junior partnership! Congratulations!" Her eyes were bright with genuine happiness.

I managed to smile, appreciative of Amanda's enthusiasm. "Thank you. It's a big decision, but I appreciate your support."

She nodded. "You've earned it. I can't wait to see where this takes you."

With a nod of thanks, I left my office. My thoughts were divided between Hannah's warm message, Denise's, and my colleagues' backing.

I navigated through the bustling city streets, and thoughts of Jack and our evening together lingered in my mind. I couldn't deny my attraction, even though we weren't dating. It added a layer of complexity to my current job situation, with the decision looming about Denise's offer.

I was thankful for the serendipitous meeting that brought him into my life in a new light. It reminded me to embrace unexpected moments and explore what they might lead to.

I arrived at the address he'd shared, surprised by the unexpected destination, a karaoke bar. Stepping out of my car, I walked up to him, and we exchanged a warm hug.

"How did you realize I would love this?" I smiled as we entered.

He chuckled, his eyes twinkling with mischief. "Well, let's just say I have ways of figuring out what makes someone tick."

I raised an eyebrow, intrigued. "Karaoke is your go-to?"

He nodded, gesturing toward the stage where a guy belted a classic rock ballad. "I thought it would be fun to unwind after a hectic week. Plus, I listened to you singing along to a tune in the car once, so I took a guess."

I laughed, remembering all the impromptu jam sessions during rush hour traffic. "I do enjoy singing."

"Tonight's your night," he said, smiling. "Pick any song you like, and I'll be your biggest fan."

We settled into our cozy corner. We perused the menu, deciding on a shared appetizer platter. The lively atmosphere and dim lighting added to the place's charm, making it like a hidden gem.

"I think we should try the garlic parmesan wings. They're supposed to be good here."

"Sounds perfect." I scanned the options. "Some loaded nachos too?"

He grinned. "You read my mind."

After placing our order with the server, Jack leaned back, eyes scanning the nearby song list on a digital screen. "What will you sing tonight?"

I chuckled. "Hmm, something classic. How about 'Don't Stop Believin' by Journey?"

Jack's eyes lit up. "Great choice! It always gets the crowd going."

"Wish me luck."

He smiled. "I don't think you need any."

I grinned and let out a small giggle. "You're probably right."

The announcer called me to the stage. I experienced the familiar thrill of performing when the music started. My voice rang out, clear and resonant, filling the karaoke bar with warmth and emotion. Each note carried a piece of my passion, drawing the attention of everyone around.

Once I finished, there was a brief silence before the room erupted into applause. I smiled, exhilaration washing over me. Glancing at Jack, I spotted a sparkle in his eyes. He applauded, leaning closer to express his surprise and appreciation for my talent.

"You were amazing! I had no idea you had such a fantastic voice!"

I blushed, thankful for his praise. "Thanks!" I experienced a rush of happiness. "I've always loved singing."

There was a buzz. He leaned in with a curious look. "Holli..." he began, his voice gentle yet filled with genuine interest, "...what are your dreams? What do you see yourself doing in the future?"

I paused, caught off guard by the depth of his question. It wasn't often someone asked me about my aspirations beyond work. I took a moment to reflect, appreciating the sincerity in his gaze.

"Well..." I started, a smile tugging at my lips, "I've always dreamed of making a difference. It's about justice and helping those who can't always help themselves. I've always loved writing, too. I'll write something that moves people, like the stories I enjoyed growing up."

He nodded, his eyes reflecting understanding. "That's beautiful, Holli. I can detect how passionate you are. I have no doubt you'll make a profound impact, whether through law or writing—or both."

I highlighted the mood and picked another song from the karaoke list. I chose "Count on Me" by Bruno Mars, and soon, the melody filled the room. I immersed myself in the music again, singing with all my passion. This time, it resonated with me.

The last notes faded, and I looked at him, curious about his reaction. His eyes were bright with admiration, and he applauded once again. "You have an incredible voice," he said. "I'm amazed by your talent."

I blushed at his praise. "Thank you," I experienced a rush of happiness. "I'm glad you enjoyed it."

We spent a few more minutes chatting and soaking in the lively atmosphere before calling it a night. Jack insisted on walking me to my car, and his thoughtful gesture made me smile. It had been an unexpected and delightful evening.

Chapter 12

A smile crossed my face as memories of dinner with Jack flooded back. The evening had been filled with delicious food, shared stories, and genuine laughter. Sipping my morning coffee, I realized today demanded a different focus.

Settling into my office chair, I prepared to tackle the tasks ahead. Three crucial tasks needed my immediate attention, each promising to define the course of my professional future. I needed to meet with the senior partners, where I would need to navigate the delicate waters of advancement.

The daunting task was confiding in Amanda, Michelle, and Steve about my plans. I had to compose an email to Denise, articulating my thoughts on the unexpected job opportunity at her sports agency.

I sat at my desk, organizing my ideas for the day ahead, when Amanda peeked into my office with a warm smile.

"Hey, Holli! How was dinner last night?" Her eyes filled with genuine curiosity.

"It was fantastic," I smiled, recalling the laughter and stories.

"I'm glad to have caught that. Any juicy details you can share?" She leaned against the doorframe.

Laughing, I said, "Plenty, but I'll have to fill you in when we have more time."

Her expression turning, "Got it. Do you need any help with today's schedule?"

I paused, shifting gears to the tasks at hand. "I was hoping you could assist me with something. Can you arrange a meeting with the senior partners later this morning? I want to handle it as soon as possible."

Amanda's demeanor shifted to one of support. "I'll take care of it, Holli. Let me know when you're ready and I'll coordinate with them."

"Thanks. I appreciate you," I said.

After a few minutes of work, she appeared again, her brisk footsteps announcing her presence. "They're waiting for you in the conference room."

"Already? That was quick." I was impressed by Amanda's efficiency.

"Yep." Her eyes reflected her readiness to support me.

"Thank you. I'll head over there now," I gathered my notes and left my office. The polished floors cooled beneath my heels as I walked down the corridor. With each step, I can sense the nervous energy. I approached the conference room. The sunlight filtered through the blinds, creating patterns on the floor. The door stood ajar, and I heard the senior partners discussing the matter inside.

Taking a breath, I pushed open the door and entered the room. The air was crisp, tinged with the scent of paper and the faint aroma of coffee that lingered from earlier. I greeted the senior partners with a confident smile, ready to dive into the important discussion ahead.

"Good morning," I stepped forward to take my place at the table.

All of them stared at me and said their good morning.

I glanced at each one of them. "I have decided on the Junior Partnership."

Thompson looked at me. "Oh? What did you decide?"

I cleared my throat. "Thank you all for this opportunity. When I first entered the legal profession, I believed in justice and wanted to impact people's lives."

I paused, gathering my thoughts as memories of my journey flooded back. "Honesty has always been one of my guiding principles," My eyes met theirs with conviction. "I must admit, in pursuit of this position, I found myself tested in ways I hadn't thought of."

I recounted how Davis had sought to manipulate my ambitions and how close I had come to compromising my values in pursuing job advancement. "Ambition, while a driving force, also exacted its toll. It cost me a relationship with a wonderful man—a reminder that balance is crucial in professional and personal pursuits."

I held their gaze. "That's why, after careful consideration. I will have have to respectfully declined the offer of a junior partnership, and this is my two-month notice. I will be leaving Winston and Associates."

There was a moment of silence, the air thick with surprise and contemplation. The senior partners exchanged glances, their expressions a mixture of curiosity and perhaps a hint of disappointment.

"May we ask why?" asked Mr. Jacobs.

I was grateful for the opportunity to explain. "I came into this profession to uphold principles I hold dear—integrity, justice, and fairness. The offer is an honor. I've realized that my path to achieving those ideals lies beyond these walls."

"Holli, we value your contributions. Are you sure about this choice? There's much we can provide you here," said Ms. Patel.

I appreciated their concern but remained steadfast. "I've thought about this extensively. I believe it's time to explore new avenues to make a difference while staying true to who I am."

Mr. Jacobs had a hint of respect in his demeanor. "We understand. Your trustworthiness and dedication have never been in question. We wish you all the best in your future endeavors."

Their acceptance and wishes lifted a weight off my shoulders. I prepared to leave the conference room. I was making the right choice for myself, and my principles.

Their understanding and support brought me peace of mind. I left the room, knowing I had made the best choice for my integrity and job path. With one task completed, the next would be the most challenging.

Making my way back to my office, I felt a mix of relief and sadness. Standing by the window, I saw the familiar cityscape.

I whispered to myself, "I'm going to miss this view."

Just then, Amanda walked in.

She looked at me with curiosity. "How did it go in there?" Her eyes searched mine for any hint of how the meeting had unfolded.

Still feeling the weight of our conversation, I smiled and said, "It went well." Then, turning to Amanda, I asked, "Could you do me a favor and ask Michelle and Steve to come to my office? I have something important to discuss with them."

She sensed the gravity of the situation. "Of course, Holli. I'll get them right away."

She left to find them. I took a moment to compose myself. This following talk was going to be difficult. I looked out the window again at my desk and tried to gather my ideas.

It wasn't long before a knock was at the door and she returned with them in tow. They looked curious and concerned, picking up on the seriousness. "Amanda, I would like you to stay too."

"Hey," Michelle said as she entered. "Amanda said you needed to talk to us?"

Steve followed, giving me a reassuring smile. "What's up?"

I gestured for them to sit and prepared to share my choice with my three closest colleagues. "Thanks for coming. I have something important to discuss."

I looked at Michelle and Steve, before speaking. "Yesterday, I was offered a junior partnership here."

Their reactions were immediate. "That's wonderful! Congratulations!" said Michelle brightly.

Steve looked impressed. "That's fantastic news! You deserve it."

I grinned, appreciating their support. "Thank you. There's more. I was also offered a position at Denise's firm Sterling & Collins Law Group."

Their expressions shifted to curiosity. Michelle tilted her head. "So, what are you going to do?"

Steve leaned forward, interested. "Do you have a decision?"

I was ready to explain. "I've thought a lot about this. My ambition almost got the best of me, I started to lose sight of why I came into this profession in the first place—to help people and to do it with integrity. Her offer is an excellent opportunity to achieve my career goals. So, I've turned down the partnership here and will accept the job with Sterling & Collins Law Group."

There was a moment of silence as Michelle and Steve processed my words. Michelle was the first to speak. "Holli, I'm proud of you. That must have been a hard choice."

Steve acknowledged. "I'm going to miss you around here."

Amanda stood, smiled, and said, "It sounds like you're selecting the best option for you. That's what matters most."

I hugged them as they left my office, turning to Steve last. "You can rent my house cheap until you and Tiffany find something you like."

He gazed at me with gratitude. "Thanks, Holli. I'm going to miss you."

I embraced him. "I'll miss you too."

A few minutes later, Amanda came back. She had tears in her eyes and hugged me. "We made a fantastic team," she said.

I fought back tears, experiencing the weight of the moment. "We did."

She left and I was alone in my office, reflecting on the changes ahead.

Task #2, the most challenging part of my day was complete. I turned back to my desk, noticing a sense of accomplishment. What was next would be the easiest—accepting Denise's job proposal. All I had to do was write the email, and a new chapter in my career would begin.

It took me quite some time because I wanted to get it right. Crafting this was a turning point. I took a moment to collect my thoughts, then began typing.

Dear Denise,

I hope this email finds you well. After careful consideration and reflection, I am delighted to accept your offer to join Sterling & Collins Law Group. I am excited to work with you and contribute to your team.

I have submitted my resignation at Winston and Associates and will be available to start in two months. Thank you again for this fantastic opportunity. I look forward to embarking on this new journey with you.

Best regards,

Holli.

Sitting back in my chair, Task #3 was done, and as I reviewed the final draft of the acceptance email to Denise, clarity settled in. Accepting Denise's job offer had been the most straightforward decision of the day.

It felt like the culmination of a series of choices prioritizing what mattered to me. What mattered was integrity, personal growth, and a meaningful impact over fleeting titles and hollow prestige.

Working with Denise at Sterling & Collins Law Group promised to be a transformative experience. Denise's reputation for fostering a collaborative and supportive environment was something I deeply admired.

I was excited about the opportunity to work under her mentorship, where my contributions would be valued and my professional development would be actively encouraged. Denise's approach to leadership aligned with my values, emphasizing ethical practices and a genuine commitment to client welfare.

I envisioned my career taking a more profound direction under Denise's guidance. The prospect of working on high-impact cases with a team that shared my dedication to justice was invigorating.

This new role would allow me to delve into complex legal challenges and contribute meaningfully to cases aligned with my core beliefs. It was an environment where my skills and aspirations could flourish and where I could make a tangible difference.

It would be a chance to work professionally with a respected mentor. I would still have two weeks at the office, but I knew they were already managing succession planning. My caseload would drop, giving me time to visit Harborview, the beautiful coastal town I would soon call home.

Acknowledgements

Writing a book is never a solitary endeavor, and I am profoundly grateful to the remarkable individuals who shaped *Pursuing Justice* into what it is today.

First, a heartfelt thank you to Riley Flanigan, Sara Davil, Tiffany Vega, and Lia Thomas. Your insights, feedback, and relentless dedication to refining this story have been invaluable. Your commitment to this project has made all the difference, and I sincerely appreciate your contributions.

To my wife, Holli—your love, support, and unwavering belief in me have been the foundation of this book. You've been my rock and my greatest source of inspiration, and for that, I am eternally grateful.

Lastly, a huge thank you to my readers. Your willingness to embark on this journey with me means more than I can express. I hope you find something in these pages that resonates with you, and my greatest wish is that you see a part of yourself in the character of Holli.

The next installment of this story will be released in January 2026. Join our community and stay updated by signing up at www.hojopresspublishing.com

About the author

John Russell is a seasoned author and expert in organizational leadership, having earned his doctorate from National University. He is the author of the acclaimed four-book Published Investigation series. He has recently expanded his literary portfolio with Stories from the Heart, a collection of five compelling short stories.

The Investigation series, inspired by John's wife and three grown daughters, began as a heartfelt Christmas gift to them, reflecting his dedication to both family and storytelling. His entrepreneurial spirit led him to establish HojoPress Publishing in December 2023, where he continues to craft and share stories that resonate with readers.

John's life is rich with personal passions beyond writing. He is an avid sports enthusiast and finds joy in his family life. He is married with three daughters and two grandchildren, and he cherishes the companionship of his basset hound. John embodies a life of creativity, leadership, and connection through his work and hobbies.

44444

Other Books From John Russell

<u>Investigation Series</u>
Friendship Unveiled
The Heroes of Centerville
Kodiak Mysteries
Clarkston Secrets

<u>Holli Series</u>
Pursuing Justice

Other Books from John Russell

Stories from the Heart
Love Songs (Spring 2025)

Be sure to follow John Russell at: Goodreads.com; BookBub.com & LinkedIn for more update on future projects and behind the scenes content.

Purchase these from:
Amazon.com
BN.com
Apple Books
Kobo.com
www.hojopresspublishing.com